GHOSTLAND 3

SHAUN WHITTINGTON

SEVERED PRESS
HOBART TASMANIA

Ghostland is a work of fiction, and many of the events in the book occur in real places. However, in these areas I have taken the liberty of exaggerating certain things that suited the book. Other places that are mentioned may not be real at all, so if you are from the area that I have written about, try not to be too upset that I have twisted a few things.

This is a book about after the apocalypse, so it does contain tension, gore, and scenes that could upset individuals, especially scenes involving children. It needs to be as real as possible, and in reality nobody would be exempt from such an unforgiving world.

Thanks,

Shaun.

The Canavars are coming, so you better hide and pray.
If you don't believe me then you're going to die today.
They'll eat your flesh, they'll eat your brains, and they'll eat your heart
and more.
The Canavars are everywhere; you better lock your door.

Tyler Washington
Aged 10

CHAPTER ONE

The broad-shouldered man's legs were becoming tired and he decided to sit on the step of the large cabin. He sat down and released a groan as his knees cracked. He was in his forties, but sometimes, especially first thing in the morning, he felt like he was in his seventies. His knees hurt, his back ached, and his neck was stiff.

It was early morning and it looked to be a nice day. It felt humid already and the sky was cloudless. Nineteen days had passed by without an incident, and that was just the way Donald Brownstone wanted it to stay. He had only seen one Canavar on his search for supplies, and that was from a distance, but he knew complacency could lead to death.

The dead had dwindled in numbers, or at least that's what it felt like, but another danger was around: Other survivors.

Over the last month or so he had heard the name Orson, his friends were burned out of their home three weeks ago by a man called Hando, and a new danger could be present that had been brought to his attention. He still hadn't forgotten the story of the meat wagons.

When the cabin was surrounded by the dead and he had fled to lead them away from the rest of the group, he saw a group of guys in a pickup, with one of them killing a Canavar. It was there he had heard the story of the meat wagons. He had no idea if the story was true. Maybe the older guys were trying to scare the young man doing his initiation test, but they certainly sounded convincing.

After twelve months of the world being the way it was, Donald didn't think cannibalism was totally far fetched, but what did intrigue him was where did these guys get their fuel from? Twelve months after the announcement on June 9th, and these guys were still driving around. Did they have a large supply back at their camp? But where was their camp? Wherever it was, it was where Orson stayed, because he heard the name being mentioned by one of the men. Wherever they stayed, it appeared that Orson was their leader.

Donald, still sitting on the step of the large cabin, brought his knees up and took a look around the greenery that surrounded him. They had supplies, but they needed to get more before the autumn kicked in. They were near a pond, so water and washing wasn't a problem. It was the lack of food that was the trouble. The produce that grew outside the now burnt out farmhouse was reluctantly allowed to grow for two more weeks, before Yoler and Dicko went up and gathered the vegetables before somebody else came across them. The potatoes especially were small and weren't given the time to flourish to a more respectable size, but the paranoia of other survivors taking the produce was too strong to leave the vegetables for another couple of weeks. After two weeks, Dicko had decided that he couldn't wait any longer. He said that if they went up there and the vegetables had been taken, they would kick themselves.

Donald could feel himself drifting away, but soon lifted his head once his eyes closed and his head dropped. He hadn't been on watch. Donald had simply woken up early, after having a nightmare about his son, and decided to get up and get some air.

Putting somebody on a night watch was something that had been discussed, but all came to the conclusion that it was too dangerous. Sitting in the darkness, surrounded by trees, would only put the life of the guard in danger. The camp was surrounded by tins with string, so if intruders, alive or dead, did enter the camp, the group would soon know about it.

A rustle to his left widened Brownstone's eyes and made him reach for the knife he had in his pocket. He gazed in the direction of where the noise had come from, and waited for whatever was about to unfold.

"Anybody there?" Donald whispered. "If so, you're with good people. No need to be alarmed."

There was no response, and a minute later Donald knew why.

Out of the woods stepped something he had been face to face with on a few occasions. It was a dog. The female dog was a black Labrador, and many moons ago Donald had owned a similar dog. This breed was normally placid, a bit over excited, and relatively harmless. This one, however, was starving. It wasn't as malnourished as some dogs he had seen in the past, but he could see the ribs of the canine. He was pretty sure that in more populated areas, especially cities, a lot of domestic pets who had lost their owners were roaming the streets, desperate to eat anything.

"Alright, boy?"

Donald had always wanted a canine companion, but every time he came across a stray dog, they were vicious, frightened and starving. This dog was no different.

The female canine lowered her head and crept towards Donald, showing its teeth, snarling.

Donald sighed and knew he had to put the animal down. He hated doing this. He stood up and took a few casual steps towards the dog, and the canine stopped moving and seemed hesitant. Donald was a big man and this desperate canine had stopped snarling. It looked like the Labrador was backing down, and Donald was relieved. He didn't want to kill the animal if he could avoid it.

The cabin door opened, startling both Donald and the dog, and the canine turned and scampered away into the woods.

"What was that?" Helen Willis scratched at her dark bobbed hair, stepped out and gave off a yawn.

"A dog," Donald said.

"Was it friendly?"

"Not really," Donald cackled and began to scan the trees, making sure there was no sign of the canine. "Given the chance, I think it would have loved to eat me, you dig what I'm sayin'?"

"Jesus," she cried.

"Nothing to worry about, Helen," Donald looked up at the woman. "Nothing I'm not used to. But I suppose it's mental to what we're now used to."

Helen sat down on the top of the cabin's step and brushed her hair back with her fingers. She leaned her elbows on her thighs and puffed out a sad breath.

"You okay?" Donald called over to her.

Helen shrugged her shoulders. "Just feeling a bit down."

"I can relate to that."

CHAPTER TWO

Dicko opened his eyes and had woken from his nightmare. He looked around and could hardly see in the dusky cabin. He could hear the sound of heavy breathing from the people who were sleeping in the cabin with him, and attempted to sit up. He had slept on the floor, and now his back was feeling the aftermath of six hours sleep on a hard floor with no protection. He sat up with difficulty and put his arms in front of him and tried to stretch. He heard part of his back crack and wondered if had overstretched. The last thing he needed was a back injury, any type of injury, in this world.

He remained sitting in the middle of the floor whilst people slept around him, and brought his knees up to his chest and wrapped his arms around his shins. He tried to clear his mind, but the nightmare he had experienced was affecting him and making his throat swell. He had had nightmares before, but this one was more like a flashback than a fictional dream. In Dicko's nightmare the incident had actually happened many months ago.

Dicko had just lost his wife and daughter, and the only thing he had left in the world was his seven-year-old son, Kyle.

It had been over two months into the apocalypse, and Dicko and his son were staying at a camp in a town called Rugeley. The camp was basically a road that had been sectioned off at each end by LGVs. The road was called Sandy Lane and the place was simply known as The Sandy Lane Camp and had many residents in the place and was still growing.

Some people lived in the houses, but farmers who had fled their farms had chosen to live on the football field, near a large building that used to be a place where people drank and where functions took place.

His eyes filled as his thoughts went back to the day he lost his son. Kyle and his father were out for a walk along the field, and Kyle announced that he needed to pee. Dicko told his son to pee in the field, but his son was too embarrassed to, and opted to use the toilets in the changing rooms. Dicko had always blamed himself for the death of the only thing he had left, and it had made him lose his mind for a few months and become unstable in his behaviour. But somehow he came back. He didn't come back as his old self. That would never happen after losing his entire family, but he did manage to claw back most of his sanity.

Paul remembered looking for Kyle, with a female friend of his, and checked everywhere possible. They checked the changing rooms, which was used back in the old world for football teams, and he felt his knees buckle when his eyes clocked his son. Somehow a stray Canavar had gotten into the camp and was inside the changing room.

Kyle had been attacked.

He was already dead when Dicko and his friend had arrived, and was being devoured by a member of the dead.

The last moments of his little boy's life had always plagued Dicko. He had lost his mind for months after. His last camp was at a place called Little Haywood. The small camp was a street that had been closed off called Colwyn Place. He left there after a few weeks, and had been on the road for months.

He stroked his dark beard that had signs of grey, especially in the chin area, and wiped his eyes.

He then thought about the people he had left behind at the camp, and then meeting a member of Colwyn Place when out on the road. Her name was Stephanie, and she was only fourteen years old.

Dicko had met up with two other survivors, but didn't realise there was a dark side to these guys. A vehicle was heard in the distance by Dicko and the two other men and saw it lose control and end up on the grassy bank. Not waiting for Dicko, the two men excitedly ran towards the motor. When Dicko finally caught up with them, after answering the call of nature, he could see the two men were abusing a young girl. It was Stephanie. She recognised Dicko straightaway, and he recognised her.

Dicko tried to persuade the two men to let her go, but they refused and turned nasty. Dicko killed them both and saved Stephanie. The young girl had been out on a run with two other females called Ophelia and Elza, but the two had been overwhelmed by the dead. Stephanie, a fourteen-year-old, was trying to drive the large vehicle back to Colwyn Place by herself. They said their farewells and that was the last time Dicko had seen anybody from that camp.

He looked around the cabin one last time and made a painful noise when trying to stand to his feet. He stretched his arms in the air, almost bending his spine in the shape of a banana, put his boots on, and then made his way outdoors. He opened the cabin door and went down the steps to the grassy area and could see Helen and Donald conversing with one another.

"Morning," Helen called over. "Sleep well?"

"Not really," Dicko groaned. "I'm stiff all over. And not in a good way either."

"You should try lying on the grass tonight," Donald chuckled. "If you look up you can see the stars, you dig what I'm sayin'?"

"I was thinking about doing that tonight," Dicko said with a straight face, stopping Donald's chuckling.

Dicko looked around where the huts used to be. When the camp had ten people, before they were attacked, there was the large cabin and some huts where people used to sleep. The cabin was a luxury, as well as safer, and the residents took turns to sleep in there. Donald had decided to remove the huts and used them as firewood over the weeks, and everybody, all seven of them, slept in the cabin.

"Are you mad?" Donald scoffed at Dicko. "Sleeping outside?"

"Why not?" Dicko hunched his shoulders. "I've done it before. This is a lot safer than what I've done in the past."

"Forget it." Helen nudged Donald and nodded over to Dicko. "He's winding you up."

"I'm not." Dicko smiled. "If I stay out here tonight, I'd be able to hear the sound of the dead coming through the woods. Stealth isn't their strong point. Plus, the camp is surrounded with our ... ahem ... alarm system. And I sleep with one eye open these days."

"Anyway, I better make a move," Helen moaned and scratched at her greasy hair. "I've got David's clothes and my hair to wash."

"Okay," Donald nodded. "I'll keep you company. Wanna go now?"

Helen nodded. "I'll try and get it done before David wakes up."

Helen went over to the cabin and crept inside. Seconds later she exited with a bunch of clothes.

"Those quilts need washing," she said. "They're starting to stink."

"We'll need to get more on the next supply trip," said Donald. "I've noticed that the evenings have been getting a bit chilly, despite it being summer. Bloody English weather."

Donald and Helen were ready to go. Donald looked at Dicko strangely and could see he was staring into space, like some madman. Donald gave Helen a gentle nudge and pointed over to Dicko and began to chuckle.

"You alright over there, Dicko?" Helen spoke up, and joined in with Donald. "You were miles away."

"Yeah." Dicko released a depressed sigh and added, "I was just thinking about Simon and Imelda."

The smiles on Helen and Donald's faces soon evaporated.

CHAPTER THREE

Gavin, Lisa Newton and her daughter, Grace, had emerged out of the cabin over the last ten minutes. They decided to collect wood for a fire. Usually, on a morning, a fire would be lit and soup would be made. With only vegetables left, the soup was going to be a vegetable one. Some other stock, situated in the corner of the cabin, was still available, but a supply run was definitely needed, and Yoler and Dicko were the ones to go once they were washed at the pond.

Yoler Sanders and young David were the only ones left in the cabin.

Out of the female and the young boy, Yoler Sanders was the first to wake up. Like Dicko, she had slept on the floor, but had a quilt doubled over and placed on the floor as a poor substitute for a mattress. The trouble was that when she woke up, she was off the quilt and was lying on the floor. She had no idea how long she had been like that, but her smarting back suggested that it had been most of the night.

She sat up and could see cracks of daylight seeping into the cabin. She was aware that everybody had gone, apart from young David, and decided to stay with the little man until he woke up. She stood up, put her boots on, and walked around the cabin, trying to limber up and reduce the stiffness. Yoler was dressed in green combats, boots, and was wearing a creased light blue T-shirt.

She sniffed her armpits and her nose twitched. This had been the worst she had smelled in months. The sooner she got to that pond and put some shower gel to good use the better. The toiletries, as well as the food, was being rationed, and she couldn't wait to go out with Dicko for a supply run. The group of people had three weeks of quiet with zero drama, but in truth, Yoler was bored and missed the action, providing she wasn't in any life threatening situations.

She was glad to be out of the camp. She loved Dicko's company. He was cheeky and since he had opened up nearly a month ago about his past, she liked him even more. He used to be a father and a husband, and she had empathy for the man that had lost everything, yet was still surviving a year after the announcement.

She heard whimpering coming from her left and could see young David's head going from side to side. It looked and sounded like he was having a nightmare. She sat next to him on the bed, and placed her hand on his forehead and shushed him gently. It didn't work and he opened his eyes and released a frightened gasp. The boy sat up and rubbed his eyes. He looked around the cabin, confused, and then gazed at Yoler.

"I think you were having a nightmare, kiddo," Yoler said with a smile.

David nodded and said, "I was having a bad dream."

"You certainly were." Yoler rubbed his head. "What was it about?"

"I was running through the woods with mummy," the boy began with little hesitation. "The Canavars were behind, following us, and I got stuck in some mud."

"Oh, that sounds terrible."

"It was very scary," he said with a nod. "The Canavars were getting closer and mummy was struggling to pull me out of the mud and I was screaming."

"Oh, that's a shame." She placed her hand on his soft cheek briefly.

"But then suddenly..." David paused and a small smile emerged on the little boy's face, "I felt these hands grab my shirt from behind. I was lifted up in the air and I was stood next to mummy."

"How did that happen?" Yoler spoke with a smile. "Was it God?"

David shook his head. "It was daddy."

"Your dad?"

"It was his ghost." David wiped his eyes and although he seemed happy when talking about his dream, his eyes were filling. "He kissed me on the forehead and then disappeared."

"And what about the Canavars?" Yoler asked, now getting a tad emotional herself.

"I don't know." David hunched his shoulders. "As soon as daddy kissed me that was when I woke up."

David then looked around the cabin, only just realising that it was just him and Yoler present. "Where's mummy?"

Yoler stood up and offered her hand to the young boy. "Outside, of course. Are you coming?"

David smiled and took Yoler's hand. The pair of them exited the cabin and could see that Gavin, Grace and Lisa were trying hopelessly to make a fire. Dicko was a few feet deep into the woods, with his back to everyone, having a pee, and Donald and Helen were coming through the trees to their left.

"Mummy!" David yelled and ran over.

Both mother and son hugged and Yoler looked at Helen and Donald with a smirk.

She said, "Where have you two been? Have you been up to any funny business?"

"Don't be silly," Helen laughed. "We were at the pond, having a wash." She then bent over and sniffed David's hair. "I think you'll be taking a trip to the pond tomorrow."

"I'm okay," said David.

"It's not up for debate," Helen laughed. "Your hair's beginning to smell a bit."

Grace, Gavin and Lisa Newton had managed to get the fire started, and Dicko emerged from the woods and mocked, "That's cheating. You used a lighter."

"So?" Grace laughed. "May as well use it if you've got it."

"Try using two flints. In fact, I used two sticks once. Took me ages."

"It's not a competition," Lisa laughed. "But you win."

Yoler went over to Dicko and gave him a playful slap, asking if he was ready to go. He nodded.

All Yoler and Dicko took with them, apart from their weapons, was one towel and some soap that would only last one wash. They said farewell to the small group and headed for the pond, eventually being swallowed up by the greenery.

"When we get to the pond," Dicko began, "the first thing I'm gonna do is strip down to my bare arse and go straight in."

"Are we still talking about the pond, Dicky Boy?" Yoler giggled.

"Yes." Dicko flashed Yoler a hard stare. "I told you weeks ago. We're just gonna have to put up with handjobs from now on, now that we don't have protection."

"Oh, you can't beat the real thing, though."

"No, but unprotected sex is too risky."

"Just pull out when you're near."

"I said no."

"Fine." Yoler pouted her lips like a child and said with a smile. "Once you are clean then maybe I'll nosh you off. You up for that?"

"Well, it's not gonna suck itself, I suppose," Dicko laughed.

"Fine, but I want you to return the favour."

"First things first." Dicko pointed up ahead and both could see the trees thinning out. They had made this journey dozens of times and were about twenty yards from the pond.

Over the last few weeks it had been a lifesaver.

Thank Christ it was there.

CHAPTER FOUR

Not for the first time, Yoler and Dicko stripped to their briefs by the pond, ready for a freezing cold wash. It wasn't so bad once they were in for a few minutes, but stepping into that water was the worst part of getting washed. David Willis cried when he had to get washed, but was getting better as the days ticked by. Dicko looked over at the other side of the pond. For weeks they went to that area to collect water, when they were staying at the farm.

"You okay?" Yoler asked him. She was in a foot of water and could see that her male friend was staring into nothingness.

Dicko nodded the once.

"You thinking about Imelda and Simes?"

"A little," he groaned. "I was thinking about going up to the farm and having a look around."

"What for?" Yoler shivered as she ran the soap over her shoulders and chest. "The only thing that's up there, since we dug out all the veg, is Simon and Imelda, resting in peace."

"Just fancied a walk around there." Dicko shrugged his shoulders. "Take a trip down memory lane. I know it was short-lived, but that was the happiest I'd been in months."

"I'll come with you."

"No." Dicko shook his head. "I'll go alone."

"Okay." Yoler had finished lathering her body and dipped herself in, up to her neck. "But don't go inside. The farmhouse is still standing, but the fire's probably weakened it and it could collapse any time."

Yoler walked out of the pond, shivering, arms wrapped around her chest. Dicko held out the towel and she took it.

"We can't do this washing malarkey in December," she huffed. "It'll freeze the piss out of us. We'll end up with pneumonia."

"Don't worry about that now," Dicko said with a snicker. "December is months away."

She passed him what was left of the soap, and the man in his forties waded through the bitterly cold water and washed his body and his beard and hair, with the rest of the soap. He dunked himself under and stood up straight so that the water came up to his nipples. After his quick wash, he returned to the grassy area where Yoler was getting dressed, and grabbed the towel off of the floor, his body shivering violently.

Yoler looked down to Dicko's groin area and laughed, "Cold in that pond, isn't it?"

"Piss off," Dicko laughed. "Anyway, the next supply run we go on, we better come across some razors. That minge of yours looks like it belongs to a Yeti."

"Cheeky cunt." Yoler sat down and began to put on her boots. "I'm doing okay, considering I haven't waxed in a year. It's not that bad. You're just being defensive because..."

Yoler had finished tying her laces and quickly stood up, picking up her machete. Dicko could see what she was looking at and quickly got dressed.

Two of the dead had stumbled through the wooded area and were now on the other side of the pond. The two dead were burnt, as if they had been set on fire. Dicko guessed that they were part of the horde that turned up at the farmhouse all those weeks ago, or had somehow been involved in another fire incident.

The dead already spotted Yoler and Dicko, but couldn't quite fathom how to get to them. They seemed reluctant to step into the water, and by the time they realised that they could reach the pair of them by walking around the pond, Yoler and Dicko were already out and dressed.

"I'll get rid of them," said Dicko, and pulled out his trench knife. "I'm going that way anyway."

"You're going to the farm now?"

"Yeah, why not?"

"Okay." Yoler sighed and said with a cheeky smirk, "I'll see you later, Paul Dickson."

He managed a chuckle and said, "Dicko will do just fine."

Dicko casually walked around the pond to meet his two aggressors and removed them with ease. He kicked one over, making it fall, and stabbed the remaining one in the side of the head. Once the stabbed creature fell to the floor, Dicko placed his boot on the chest of the one that he had kicked over, stopping it from getting to its feet, and shoved his blade into its right eye socket. Once the blade was pulled out, he wiped it on the grass and put it back into its holster. He looked at the two bodies and decided to drag them into the woods on his way back, out of sight.

He strolled through the cluster of trees and was out on a large field within a minute.

He stopped walking and a small smile was produced. He looked at the farmhouse, but there was sadness behind that smile also.

He made his way across the field and the memories came flooding back. His feet hit the incline of the hill and once he reached the top, he looked up and gazed at the burnt out place. He then looked to his left and could see the small barn and the drive where they used to park the Mazda.

The car was still sitting there, burnt out. In front of him were the vegetable patches Yoler had worked hard on, although there was nothing there now. To his right were the two graves of Simon and Imelda. Thankfully the graves hadn't been damaged by individuals or wild dogs. Even Imelda's cuddly toy Lambie was still present by the cross.

Dicko was feeling emotional and turned to look at the house once more.

Despite what Yoler had said to him earlier, he was going in.

CHAPTER FIVE

Lisa Newton and Gavin were sat on the top step of the cabin and watched as young Grace and Helen were gathering sticks to make a little camp for David. What they didn't tell him was that, like the huts before, his camp would probably have to be dismantled and used as firewood.

"He seems to be a lot cheerier these days," Gavin said to Helen, referring to the little boy.

"I know."

Lisa smiled as her daughter, Grace, playfully ruffled the boy's hair, and left the grassy area to go into the woods a foot deep to get more sticks and branches. She told Grace not to go in too deep, but they could all see in the woods for many yards. It was clear. And by the time winter arrived, there wouldn't be a leaf left on any tree, and they'd be able to see danger coming from a long way away.

"When I returned here with Grace," Gavin continued, "he hardly spoke."

"He's had a rough ride," said Lisa.

"When it was the ten of us," Gavin spoke with a reminiscing smile, "the lad was in decent spirits. Then we were attacked and we all split up. Some of us died."

"Helen told me what happened during your absence. That young boy had lost his little friend and her father died as well."

"Simon," Gavin said with a nod. "I only met him once. David had gone AWOL and Donald, Helen and myself went looking for him. He was at the pond where Simon, Yoler, Dicko and Imelda were."

Lisa cleared her throat and gazed at her daughter with sad eyes. "I can't thank you enough for what you did, looking after my daughter."

"I know. A strange one that I bring her back to this place and you and Donald are here. Not sure whether it was luck or fate."

"My other daughter didn't deserve the death she had. She was only fourteen, for Christ's sake. I just wish I had the chance to bury her."

Gavin released a depressed sigh and placed his hand on Lisa's thigh. "What you and your daughters went through should never have happened."

"And yet that bastard is still out there. That Hando character."

"There's no justice in the world, is there? You killed one of them, Dicko and the rest killed another and chopped another man's hand off, which probably killed him, but the leader escapes without a scratch."

The two continued to look in the direction of Helen, Grace and little David, and a silence covered them briefly. Grace looked over to her mum and gave her a wide smile.

Gavin also smiled, but soon lost it and cocked his head to one side as if he had seen something through the trees. Not taking any chances, Gavin stood up and walked down the cabin's steps.

"Where are you going?" Lisa asked him.

"I thought I heard something."

Gavin picked up a three-foot branch from the floor, despite having a knife in his pocket, and walked over to Helen, Grace and David, telling them to get back inside the cabin.

"What is it?" Helen asked.

"He thinks he heard something." Lisa Newton approached the four of them and pulled out a knife and looked at Gavin. "I'll come with you."

"But..."

"I'm no stranger to violence, Gavin. I'm coming with you."

Gavin sighed in defeat and said, "Come on then."

He watched Helen, Grace and the confused little boy go into the cabin, and the pair of them reluctantly walked through the trees. It was clear enough, and the two could see ahead of them and to the side, but it was still eerie being in the woods, knowing that there was a presence near them, somewhere.

The two of them never exchanged a word as they progressed deeper. Gavin was in two minds whether to just go back to the camp and keep an eye out, but then he released a gasp when a female appeared from behind a tree, like something out of a horror movie, and just stared at the two of them from around thirty yards.

Gavin and Lisa stopped walking and Gavin held his hand up, letting the female know that they were friendly. The female began to walk backwards and seemed to be unsure of the two individuals.

"It's okay," Gavin spoke up. "We won't hurt you. We have a place not far from here."

"I know," the female said. "I've seen it."

"Let's talk," Lisa decided to speak up, hoping that the presence and the voice of another female would relax the stranger. "My name's Lisa, and this is Gavin. We're just trying to survive, just like you. There's a few more back at our place, including a little boy."

The strange woman had long dark greasy hair and was wearing sports attire that had seen better days. She looked confused and said, "You're not people from the wagons, are you?"

"The ... the wagons?" Lisa looked genuinely confused and the stranger could see this.

"The meat wagons. You're not with them, are you?"

"We have no idea what you're talking about."

Gavin decided to take a step forwards and Lisa did the same. Gavin dropped the branch and raised his hands as a 'I come in peace' gesture and Lisa copied him. The woman now looked relaxed and sat down, against a tree. Lisa and Gavin continued to walk until they were near the woman. Lisa and Gavin decided to sit down, opposite the woman, and also had their backs against a different tree.

The woman gave off a timid smile and announced, "I've been out in the countryside for a while now."

Lisa asked, "How long?"

"Not sure." The woman elevated her shoulders and thought for a few seconds. "A few weeks ... maybe. Sometimes a week can feel like a month, so I'm not sure."

"Have you always been on your own?" Lisa continued to probe and Gavin decided to keep quiet. He thought that she would open up better talking to another woman.

"No." The woman dipped her head with sadness and added, "I was with my husband and son."

"Oh," was all Lisa could muster. She knew there was going to be a heartbreaking story that involved the woman's husband and her child, and allowed the woman to pour her heart out in her own time.

"We were walking along the main road. We reached an orchard and decided to pick some apples. We hadn't eaten in three days, so when we came across this we were delighted. But then we saw a man walking along the road and he waved at us. He seemed friendly, just like you two, but then he pulled out a walkie-talkie, spoke into it, and a few seconds later a van or a truck came from around the corner. I think it was a large white Transit van, but for some reason people nickname them the meat wagons." She shook her head and laughed at herself, realising she was going off on a tangent. "Anyway, this van pulled up and two men jumped out the back. My son was grabbed and another man clubbed my husband. They threw them into the back of the van and the man with the walkie-talkie ran after me, obviously trying to get me in the back of the van with them. I ran. I ran so hard, but I had no choice."

"Of course," Lisa said, and could see the woman was becoming emotional. "You had to."

"That was the hardest thing I ever had to do. Run away and leave my family behind." The woman cried, "You know, I could hear my son crying as I ran away."

Lisa stood up, went over to the woman and crouched down and touched her shoulder. "If you'd stayed, you would have died as well."

"I know." The woman wiped her eyes with the palms of her hands. She then quickly stood up and brushed herself down. "You do realise what these meat wagons are for, don't you?"

"I can guess. I heard about them from another survivor, before my family were taken away. They're cannibals. They take people and they eat them."

"Try not to think about it now."

"Just stay away from the roads," the woman said. "And be wary of strangers."

"We've never come across anything like that," said Lisa, and turned to Gavin. "Have you?"

"No." He shook his head. "But then again, I've spent most of my time in the woods with my camp."

Lisa could see the woman was about to leave and asked her where she was going.

"I'm sorry to have bothered you," the woman said, "but I'm better off on my own."

The woman began to run away, further into the woods before Lisa could respond.

"Come back!" Lisa began to yell. "At least let us feed you before you go!"

"Leave it," Gavin said and stood up straight.

Lisa watched helplessly as the woman eventually disappeared. She shook her head and turned to look at Gavin.

He said, "Well, that was weird."

CHAPTER SIX

He crept through the house with his t-shirt over his nose. The smell of burning plagued the house and he stood at the bottom of the stairs. He looked up and shook his head. There was no point going up. Nothing could have survived the fire.

He thought taking a walk in the place would ignite the few memories that he had, but he felt nothing. The memories that he had weren't inside the four walls of this decrepit house, they were in his head. He sighed and walked through the living room and into the kitchen. He stepped out of the place and could see Yoler Sanders standing with her hands on her hips, and the machete tucked into the belt she had on.

"I thought you were going back to the camp," Dicko laughed.

"I was just passing," she joked. "Anyway, it's boring back at the camp. It's all washing clothes and making soup and filtering water."

"Has to be done."

"Yeah, well it bores the piss out of me."

Dicko lowered his head and shook it. "You know what your problem is, don't you?"

Yoler smiled. "Why don't you tell me?"

Dicko walked over to the two graves and Yoler slowly followed him. He stood and gazed at Simon and Imelda Washington's graves and began to speak.

He said, "The trouble with you is that you've spent the best part of the year fighting, surviving and killing."

"And?" Yoler giggled. "What's your point, Dicky Boy?"

"We had a few good weeks on the farm, before it went tits up," he began to explain. "And since we've moved into the woods, nothing has happened for three weeks. No drama, no Canavars ... nothing."

"So...?"

"You're bored, Yoler. I think you actually miss the violence."

"Would you think less of me if I agreed with you?"

"Of course not. I'm no different. I've been in situations where I've been face to face with the dead and had to kill the living. Shit, months ago, when I was staying at that place that I left, we were under attack by some gang. I stabbed the driver of a pickup to death, took the vehicle and drove through the gates of the camp, and ran two of the gang members over and shot another one with a shotgun that was inside the truck."

"Wow, Dicky Boy." Yoler smiled and moved closer to her male companion. "Now that I would have liked to have seen."

"It's a rush," said Dicko. "No doubt about it. But your luck will run out one day. Embrace the boredom."

"I can't," Yoler laughed. "When I'm bored I get horny. And what's a girl to do after she's given herself a good finger blasting?"

"You really do have a way with words, don't you?"

"I just hate being bored." She looked up to the cloudless sky and smiled as the sun's rays touched her face. "I remember one time, back in the early days, I stayed at this place in the countryside. My god, I had never been so bored in all my life. I decided to go north after robbing some poor guy, but at least the food kept me going for a good week."

"What do you mean?" Dicko was perplexed by her short story. "You actually robbed a poor survivor?"

"Not like that," she said, knowing what Dicko was getting at. "I think he was recruiting for a nearby camp he had. He came into the room where I was sleeping, and asked if I wanted to join him. He left his bag of goodies and went out. He said he'd be back later, but I took the bag, barricaded the room, and left through the bedroom window."

"Poor guy." Dicko shook his head at Yoler, like a disappointed father.

"Poor guy? He was a dick. I mean, what kind of person, in the middle of the apocalypse, walks around with a hockey stick?"

Dicko narrowed his eyes and turned his head to the side. "Hockey stick?"

Yoler nodded.

He ran his fingers through his beard and asked his female companion, "Where was this place that you were staying?"

"Milford, I think you call it."

"And this guy with the hockey stick. Did he give you his name?"

She nodded. "Craig ... something."

"Was it Craig Burns?"

"Shit, yeah." Yoler folded her arms and looked at Dicko suspiciously. "How...?"

"He was from the camp I was at. I left soon after he arrived." Dicko scratched his head and was finding the information difficult to process in his head. "That means, at one point, you and I were only two miles from one another. If you had agreed to join Craig, we would have met a lot sooner."

"Oh, right." Yoler didn't seem as excited as Dicko, and her lack of interest was clear on her face. "He did say something that I would never forget."

"What's that?"

"I asked him if that camp had guns, and he replied, we don't need guns, we have a Pickle."

Dicko burst out laughing and placed his hand over his mouth as soon as Yoler finished her sentence. She thought his behaviour was strange, but never bothered to query him further. Instead, she looked down on the two shallow graves, and as Dicko's laughter began to diminish, her thoughts went to Simon and Imelda.

She sighed and looked down at the two graves. "I miss them. I miss them both."

"Me too."

"I sometimes wonder..." Yoler never finished her sentence and both individuals turned around when they heard a noise behind them.

Dicko looked at the individual who created the noise and said, "I've seen you before."

The man that they were staring at was five-six in height, in his fifties, with a grey beard. He was dressed in dirty blue jeans, a cardigan was over a black T-shirt he had on. The first time Dicko had seen the man was when he was driving around the countryside looking for Simon, after they had fled from a gang and were separated.

"Can I help you?" Dicko asked the man.

The man in his fifties smiled and shook his head. "Nobody can help me."

Yoler remained silent as Dicko walked over to the man. The man didn't seem intimidated by Dicko or Yoler, when he thought it was clear that they both had weapons. The man turned and gazed at the farmhouse and puffed out a sad breath.

"A shame about this place," he said.

"I know." Dicko stood next to the man and folded his arms.

"How on earth did it happen?"

"Sabotage," Dicko replied. "Someone set fire to it."

Dicko could see the man turn in the corner of his eye and felt his gaze.

The man with the grey beard asked, "And why would someone do that?"

"They wanted what we had." Dicko decided to keep the story short with little detail. "They couldn't have it, so they tried to burn it and kill everybody inside."

"That sounds like the work of a very dangerous man."

"There're plenty of them out there, I'm afraid."

"I know. That's why I prefer to be on my own, but you guys seem okay." The man cleared his throat and asked Dicko, "So you used to stay here?"

"Briefly. I was taken in by a kind man and his little girl."

"And where are they now?"

Dicko looked to his right and pointed over to the two shallow graves.

"Oh." The man lowered his head sadly.

"I've seen you before," Dicko said to the man.

"I know. I remember. I've never left the area."

Dicko was ready to go back to the camp and say farewell to the man. The conversation was lacklustre and trying, and he could also hear Yoler impatiently huffing in the background.

"Anyway, I better go," Dicko said, and was unsure whether to invite the man back to the camp. He decided not to and pointed at the farmhouse. "You're welcome to it."

"Thanks." The man began to laugh. "But it was mine in the first place."

Dicko looked at the man strangely and the stranger began to explain.

He said, "This was my place for many years. Me and my wife stayed here. Then there was that announcement on June 9th, and then the dead came."

"How did you manage to survive so long?"

"We just stayed indoors. Months later it was the starvation that forced us out. I went out one day, trying to get supplies, and then I returned and found the place was empty. My wife had disappeared."

"What the hell happened?"

"At the time I didn't know." He hunched his shoulders. "Then a month later, when I was out, I saw her hanging from a tree."

"Jesus."

"She was in despair before I left. She wasn't coping well. A part of me thinks that she killed herself, but she didn't want me to find her body at home and put me through that."

Dicko began, "Listen, we have a camp—"

"I walk alone." The man turned and smiled at Dicko. "But thanks for the offer."

Dicko decided not to ask any further questions and looked over to Yoler. He moved his head, suggesting that they were going. He then turned to the man in his fifties and held out his hand.

"Is that you off?" the man asked.

Dicko nodded and could see that Yoler was already slowly making her way down the hill. "That's right."

The man shook Dicko's hand. "Tony Parsons."

Dicko smiled. "Paul Dickson."

"Take care, Paul."

"You too, Tony."

Dicko walked away and left the man on his own to reminisce.

He caught up with Yoler and put his arms around her shoulder. They cleared the hill and were now on the flat field. Minutes later and they had arrived at the pond.

21

CHAPTER SEVEN

The sticks on the fire were crackling and the huge pot on the stove was bubbling. It was early afternoon; Helen had made a vegetable soup and everybody was famished after having nothing to eat since the day before. They didn't wait for Yoler and Dicko, and decided to tuck right in as David had been moaning for hours that he was starving. With a jar of filtered water shared and passed amongst them, they had a bowl of soup each, served in ceramic bowls and spoons that hadn't been cleaned in days. Helen noticed that Lisa and Gavin were acting strangely since they had returned from the woods. At first, she thought that maybe some sexual activity had occurred between the pair of them, but as the minutes went by, she thought it was something else.

They finished their soup and piled the bowls and spoons together, stating that a trip to the pond to boil water and wash the utensils and bowls would have to occur before people started picking up bugs.

David was clearly bored and told his mum that he wanted to go into the cabin and work on a comic he was making. He still had crayons, a pencil, and a pad of A4 paper Donald had brought back from a run a week ago, and Helen kissed her boy and told him to go ahead and watched as he returned to the cabin. David kept the cabin door open, as the light wasn't that great, and the boy began to scribble with the adults some ten yards away or so, sitting around the fire. Lisa took the pot off the stove, in case the soup burnt and stuck to the bottom, and placed it on the grass with the lid on top, the fire still burning.

Grace, Lisa, Gavin, Helen and Donald were sitting around the fire and were all silent. Helen looked over her shoulder to see if David was still scribbling away inside the cabin. She then turned and stared at Lisa and Gavin.

"Okay," Helen sighed. "What's going on?"

Lisa and Gavin looked at one another, and Donald had no idea what she was talking about.

"What do you mean?" Donald said to Helen.

"Not you, Donald." Helen nodded at Lisa and Gavin. "These two. They've been acting strangely since they returned from the woods."

Young Grace shook her head and was fearing the worst. Had her mother and Gavin, a man she had a crush on, been at it in the woods?

"We were going to tell you," Gavin spoke up. "We were waiting until David was out of the way. We didn't want to frighten the boy. There's enough out there as it is to give the boy nightmares."

"Gavin," Donald groaned. "What are you talking about?"

Gavin looked at Lisa and she decided to be the storyteller.

"We met a woman in the woods," Lisa said. "She looked..."

Lisa didn't really know how to explain what the woman looked like.

"She looked lost, scared, and emotionally ruined," Gavin said. "She needed help."

"Anyway," Lisa took over the reins once again, "she told us her story and mentioned something about the meat wagons. Apparently, men in a vehicle turned up and took away her husband and son."

"Meat wagons?" Donald spoke with a scowl. This was something he had heard before.

"Whoever goes out on runs from now on, they need to keep away from the main road, especially if an engine can be heard in the distance."

"What are these ... meat wagons?" Grace asked. She was shaking with nerves and already knew that the explanation was going to frighten her. Even the name 'meat wagon' sent a shiver down her vertebrae.

"Cannibals," Donald said sharply. He could see Lisa and Gavin looking at him, wondering how he knew, so he decided to speak up and explain himself. "Not sure how many there are or how many vehicles they have, but there's a group of people out there ... somewhere ... that drive around and kidnap people, you dig what I'm sayin'?"

"Kidnap them?" young Grace questioned. "What for?"

All four looked at Grace and already knew the answer.

Donald continued, "Meat wagons. Cannibals. I think it's easy enough to work out."

"So..." Grace was finding the information hard to process. "So ... these meat wagon people are eating others?"

"Looks that way."

"And how do *you* know about this?" questioned Helen.

"A few weeks ago, I was out," Donald began. "In fact, it was just after the cabin was surrounded when I slipped through the side door. It was the same night." Donald cleared his throat and added, "I was at the side of the road and some guys pulled up in a pickup and killed a Canavar. They were men of Orson's, and they mentioned the meat wagons."

"Again," Helen huffed and glared at Donald, "why didn't you tell us?"

"I didn't want to cause unnecessary panic, you dig what I'm sayin'? Wasn't sure if it was just rumour talk. But now that these have bumped into that woman..."

"We better tell Dicko and Yoler," Grace said. "They go on more runs than anybody. You should have said something sooner, Donald."

"Why?" Donald shook his head and said, "It's an unwritten rule that when you hear an engine, you hide anyway."

A rustle could be heard from the side of them. Neither of them was alarmed by this. They knew it was Dicko and Yoler.

The two appeared from out of the trees and raised their hands as a silent salutation.

"You guys okay?" Dicko asked, checking out their sombre faces.

"Yeah," said Yoler. "You guys look like somebody has just shot your dog."

Donald stood up and the rest of the people around the fire did the same.

"Are you guys still going out in the morning?" Helen asked the pair of them.

"Yeah, why?" Yoler was uncomfortable about the way they were behaving. "What the piss is going on?"

Donald said, "There's something you need to know."

CHAPTER EIGHT

Next day

With an empty rucksack each, Yoler and Dicko said their farewells to the rest of the group and walked into the woods. They were out of the woods and on the main road within fifteen minutes. They had been told the story about the meat wagons, but Dicko had told the group not to worry and that he always hid whenever an engine could be heard in the distance anyway.

He believed the story, but he wasn't overly concerned about it. He was convinced that it was only desperate people who hitchhiked that probably became victims of these so-called wagons. Yoler was also unconcerned, and it was a story that wasn't mentioned between the pair of them as they walked, unaware of where they were going.

"What's up with you?" Yoler asked her quiet companion.

"Nothing."

"Nothing?" she laughed. "You've got a face like a smacked arse. Something's wrong."

"A memory appeared in my head," Dicko admitted. "It took me by surprise, that's all."

"Memories? About your kids?"

"Actually, no." Dicko smiled thinly and waggled his head. "I was thinking about my wife, Julie."

"Your wife?" Yoler giggled and tried to joke, "Were you reminiscing about when you used to spit-roast her over the marital bed?"

"Show some compassion for once," Dicko moaned at his female companion, unimpressed with her attitude. "Fuck's sake."

"Okay." Yoler lost her smile and adopted a sombre look, aware that she had spoken out of turn and that her joking was bad timing. Instead of apologising, something she wasn't good at, she asked, "What was the memory?"

"Julie had a row with our neighbours, Robert and Daisy, so the man from next door put up a large fence. We made up eventually."

"How did that happen?"

Dicko shushed her and held his hand up. They both stopped walking and looked ahead. The road ahead was winding and the woods were to either side. They could see a sign up ahead and it looked like a small village wasn't far away.

"Did you hear something?" Yoler asked her male companion.

Dicko simply nodded and never answered her verbally.

They waited and looked ahead. Yoler was unsure whether the noise that Dicko had heard was from the left or the right-hand side of the woods. She never bothered to ask.

Two men stepped out of the woods and immediately turned and clocked Dicko and Yoler standing in the middle of the road.

Both men were six feet in height and had on camouflage clothes and heavy boots. They were dressed the same, but one was rotund and the other man looked almost anorexic. They were five car lengths from Yoler and Dicko and seemed reluctant to approach them. Both of them were carrying baseball bats.

"Where you headed?" the rotund man called over.

Dicko didn't want to be rude, but he didn't want to give too much away either. "We're just on the road, my friend. Trying to survive."

"Same here," the man laughed. "You have a camp?"

Dicko looked at Yoler, who timidly shook her head at him, then turned to the two men and told them that they didn't.

"You can join us, if you want."

"Join you?"

The rotund man continued to talk and said, "We have a place, not far from here."

The rotund man was given a nudge by his malnourished-looking companion, telling him to shut up. The two of them turned to one another and began to bicker. Yoler and Dicko looked on awkwardly and waited for the two men to finish their exchange of words.

Once they were done, the large man, who looked embarrassed, said farewell to Yoler and Dicko and apologised.

"What are you sorry for?" Yoler spoke up, confused by the man's apology.

"I've said too much," the rotund man said. "It's not really up to me who can join or not. I was just getting a little excited. Apart from the people back at my camp, we don't normally see other folk."

"Okay, that's enough," his thin companion said. He raised his hand at Yoler and Dicko and said, "We need to be going. Best of luck, guys."

The two men began to walk to the other side of the road. It looked like they were entering the woods on the right side.

"Oh, and by the way." The large man called over to them and pointed to where they had just come from. "Don't bother going that way, especially if you're looking for supplies."

"Nothing there?" Dicko asked.

"No, there isn't. Plus, there's a herd of the dead not too far away. About twenty of them."

The two of them disappeared into the greenery and Dicko thanked them for the warning.

He turned to Yoler and she asked him, "Now what?"

"Straight ahead." Dicko pointed in front of him. "I was thinking of going that way anyway."

"It's a village up ahead, meaning more people and potential Canavars."

"Also means that there could be food." Dicko began to walk and Yoler stayed by his side. "Better not go too far. Even if we find a shit load of supplies and fill your bags, it's not gonna last that long with eight mouths to feed. And I'm not too sure it's worth trying to grow shit this time of year."

They could see that the road was getting steep and moaned as they made their way up. The road began to straighten and flatten, and they could both see that the village could be seen to their left. There was a main road that ran by the side of the village. It dipped and then inclined, and most of the place was situated at the bottom of the road where it dipped. The pub was up ahead, at the top of the hill, and the residential part was mainly in the area where the road was at its lowest point. It was almost as if a massive crater was there before and the village had been built at the bottom of it.

They went by the sign that stated: "Welcome to Trongate" and could see seven or eight streets, a pub, a primary school and a newsagents. The place was lucky to have had a population of seven hundred in the old world. But now...

"What do we check out first?" Yoler sighed.

Dicko hunched his shoulders and said, "The pub? If there's anything in there, which I doubt, then there'd be no point trying out the houses if we can fill our bags."

"If you say so." She nodded in the direction of the pub and they could both see that some of the windows had been smashed in. "Doesn't look good though, does it? Probably was raided in the first week, last year."

"May as well try anyway."

"Okay." Yoler sounded less than enthusiastic.

"Shall we?"

CHAPTER NINE

"Make sure you don't let her out of your sight," Lisa Newton warned Gavin.

Gavin and Grace, after their little scare earlier, had decided to go mushroom and berry picking, whilst Lisa and Helen washed some clothes as well as themselves. Helen was weak in this new world, but Donald knew she was in good hands with Lisa by her side. It was only a short trip to the pond, but he still worried. Helen and Lisa left with a bag full of dirty clothes, and Donald sat on the step of the cabin, next to young David, and watched Gavin and Grace walk into the woods with an old carrier bag that had seen better days.

Gavin screwed the carrier bag up and put it into his pocket and took out his knife from the opposite one.

"Have any idea where these berries could be?" Grace asked.

"Nope." Gavin began to laugh.

"But you've stayed here for a while now, on and off."

"I know, but we rarely went walking into the woods," Gavin said. "I suppose, in the beginning, we didn't need to. We had a decent amount of supplies, but now..."

"So you have no idea?"

"We won't go far." Gavin smiled at Grace, knowing she was feeling agitated and confused by his behaviour, so he tried to explain. "Look, I hate hanging around that place. It's so boring. And who knows? We may come across something."

Their walk continued for another three minutes and they constantly looked to their side, in front, and behind them. Aware that a lack of concentration could cost them their lives, their frantic looking continued until Gavin stopped suddenly. Grace did the same and asked what was wrong.

"Can you see what I can see?" he said with a smile.

"Um ... no." Grace ran her fingers through her greasy hair and asked Gavin, "Why are we stopping?"

Gavin pointed up ahead and said, "Look."

Grace stared in the direction of where the finger was pointing and shrugged her shoulders. "It's another tree. So what?"

"Look up."

Grace did as she was told, and saw the apples that hung off the branches of the tree that they were in front of.

"Shit." Grace's eyes widened and she ran over to it.

"Wait up." Gavin put his knife away and added, "I don't think they should be picked until late summer to early autumn."

"You seriously want to wait?"

"Probably not." Gavin walked over to Grace and could see she was about to climb up it. "I'm sure they're still edible."

He took out the carrier bag from his pocket and opened it out. He watched as she climbed higher and he told her to shake the branch, but she insisted on picking them one by one. Gavin stayed on the ground and opened out the carrier bag, ready for Grace to drop the apples into it.

"Be careful!" Gavin called up.

Grace had managed to pick two apples and dropped them. Gavin moved around with the opened bag and managed to catch them.

"This is taking forever," he moaned. "Just shake the bloody branch."

"Just let me do it *my* way." Grace began to climb across a thick branch and Gavin wasn't sure if the branch would be able to take her weight. She dropped three more into Gavin's bag and ten minutes later the bag was full and Grace was now on the ground, exhausted.

She reached into the bag that Gavin was carrying and pulled out one of the apples and took a bite.

"Tastes alright," she mumbled with her mouth full.

"Oi, that's the camp's stash," Gavin said, but she could see he was joking.

"Hang on." She took another bite and added, "I worked for these bad boys. I earned at least one apple. Helen never goes out on supply runs."

"Helen has uses in other departments." Gavin wasn't joking anymore. He was annoyed that Grace was berating Helen, and felt that it was his duty to defend the woman that he cared for.

"Oh." A smile crept onto Grace's face and this made Gavin suspicious.

"What?"

"You have a thing for Helen, don't you?"

"Me?" Gavin shook his head. He cared for Helen, but he had no desire to be her partner, although he would have been lying if he claimed that he had never fantasised about having sex with her. "Donald has a thing for her. Not me."

"Are you sure about that?"

She took another bite and Gavin reached to grab the apple she had now half eaten.

"Get off," she moaned.

He went to grab the apple again and she moved away. He walked forwards with the bag, towards Grace, and she giggled as he tried to playfully grab the apple again. She ran a few yards and he ran after her.

She giggled and ran through the woods. Gavin followed with the heavy carrier bag in his right hand.

She veered left and he did the same, now both of them laughing. She almost tripped over a large tree root and Gavin decided to run to the side and began to make growling noises, making the girl scream. Grace laughed and turned to the side and could see that Gavin had disappeared.

She stopped running and was panting hard. She gazed around the wooded area and couldn't see Gavin at all.

"Very funny, Gavin," she said. "Where are you?"

"Down here," came a timid voice.

She screwed her face in befuddlement and walked in the direction of where the voice had come from. Her feet continued to wade through the bracken and stopped when she came across a large ditch. It was around six feet in length and in width, and almost eight feet in depth. She looked down and could see Gavin was down there, the apples scattered along the floor.

"Are you hurt?" Grace asked him.

"Not really," Gavin called up. "I'm surprised I didn't break my leg."

"What the hell is this?"

"No idea. It looks man made."

Grace lay on her stomach and tried to reach down.

Gavin didn't even attempt to reach up. He knew it was useless and Grace certainly didn't have the strength to pull him up.

"Go and get Donald," he called up.

"The ditch is too deep."

"I know, but he's got some rope back in the cabin. Go get him."

"Okay."

"And be quick. This is creepy as hell."

"Be back as soon as I can."

Grace turned and ran through the woods, heading for the camp. She didn't know how far they had walked and wasn't the fittest, but was sure that she could run there without stopping.

CHAPTER TEN

They walked around the perimeter of the pub before going inside, and found nothing untoward apart from some broken windows. They were certain that people had already been here. Whether it was last week or months ago, people had definitely been here, which possibly meant that the owners no longer resided in the establishment.

No words were exchanged between the male and female, and as soon as the circumference of the pub had been completed, Dicko tried the main door. Both weren't surprised that it was open.

"Shall we?" Dicko said with a smile.

Yoler was the first to step inside and Dicko had a quick look behind him before entering.

They made sure the door was shut behind them and looked around in the dim room. It was a place that Dicko had never been in, but was aware that, like most pubs, it had living arrangements upstairs and there was a cellar somewhere.

"I think the best thing we can do is check the kitchen and the cellar," Dicko said to his female companion. "There won't be anything upstairs."

They made careful steps across the lounge area of the pub, and Dicko stopped once he clocked a door with a round window. He pointed at the door and they both made their way over. They weren't expecting anything when they walked inside. In fact, Dicko was convinced that the pub would be barren of food, and their only hope of supplies would be to scrounge from the scraps that could be available from the houses of the small village. Even if they returned to the camp with a handful of tins, the journey would be worth it.

Dicko was the first to push open the swing door and peered inside the place. It seemed clear, and he stepped inside with Yoler behind him. The place looked like it had already been ransacked, and as he approached the large refrigerator, he already knew there wasn't going to be anything edible. He opened the fridge and twisted his nose at the little rotten food that was left inside.

"Nothing," he sighed.

Yoler looked to her side and walked through the water-soaked room from the freezer that had been defrosted.

"What now?" Yoler huffed. "The cellar?"

Dicko nodded and they both left the kitchen, now looking for the cellar.

"There." Dicko pointed at a wooden door that they never noticed before. It was situated five yards to the right of the main door.

Dicko walked over to the door and tried the handle, expecting it to be locked. He placed his ear against the door, but could hear nothing. He tried the handle and surprisingly the door opened. His heart sank as the door being open told him that somebody, probably the owner, had already been into the cellar.

He pushed the door open wider, expecting there to be nothing left, and could see a set of steps and a flat ramp-like incline to the left of the steps, probably used for the transportation of beer barrels, and both were reluctant to go in. The place was pitch black and Dicko looked at Yoler, wanting a reaction.

"No way in piss am I going down there," she said.

"Okay." Dicko rubbed his head, agreeing with her blunt comment. "We'll try and find a candle or something."

Yoler, with her machete still tucked in her belt, went behind the bar and went through a set of drawers.

Dicko remained standing by the open cellar door and called over to his female companion, "Anything?"

"No candle," she said. "But I found a lighter."

"Good. At least that's something we can take back to the camp."

Yoler made her way over and flicked the lighter. It lit straightaway, and she adjusted it to increase the flame. She stepped into the cellar and they could now see inside. Two barrels sat at the left of the room, a huge wine rack was situated across the back wall, and boxes of peanuts and crisps were stacked up to the right of them.

"Good." Dicko nodded, slipped the rucksack off his shoulder, and said further, "Not the healthiest of stuff, but looks like we'll be going back to the camp with two full bags."

"Ouch!" Yoler yelled as the flame from the lighter licked her finger.

"Give it here," Dicko demanded.

"I'll see if there's a candle in the bar area," she said.

She left Dicko alone in the cellar and walked through an alcove to the bar area. She turned a corner and stopped suddenly, revealing a gasp. Her eyes widened and she froze with fear.

By the bar were a group of Canavars, fifteen in all, and two of them reacted quickly and grabbed a hold of Yoler Sanders before she had chance to pull out her machete.

She released a yell and head butted one of them that had a hold of her shirt, and she then scrambled away from the bar area. She looked over her shoulder and could see all were behind and unusually quicker than what she had been used to. She took a quick look in the cellar to see Dicko by the wine rack. Should she go in? Leave him in there and flee? She had a second to make a decision and stepped inside the cellar and slammed the door shut, sliding the bolt across.

"What the fuck are you doing?" Dicko yelled.

"Canavars," she gasped.

"How many?"

She gulped. "Loads."

The sound of hands slapping the door occurred and the noise quickly increased.

"There was more than half a dozen," Yoler said. "I hope that door holds out."

"Me too."

"What do we now?"

Dicko hunched his shoulders and shook his head.

"Not the answer I was hoping for, Dicky Boy."

Dicko, still holding the lighter, told Yoler to fill her bag. She did as she was told and he did the same.

He turned the lighter off, as it was burning his thumb, and said to Yoler, "We just need to wait until it's clear. Then we'll make a run for it."

"How do we know when it's clear?"

"When the banging stops."

"We know how persistent these cunts can be. And what if it never stops?"

"I don't wanna think about that right now."

CHAPTER ELEVEN

Gavin Bertrand looked around the ditch to see if there was any way he could climb out. There were no stray roots to grab hold of and trying to climb it by simply grabbing clumps of dirt was impossible. It took him four attempts to realise this. He had no choice. He had to simply wait, and had no idea how long it would take for Grace to get back to the camp. She couldn't get lost. It was impossible. They walked in a straight line, almost, and were conscious about heading out too far.

He wiped his hands on his jeans and looked around the decent sized hole he was stuck in. It was definitely man made, but he had no idea what it was for and if it was created before or after the apocalypse.

"Come on, Grace."

Gavin couldn't stand still.

He was pacing the bottom of the ditch nervously and began to think about the other people who used to be in his small community. Apart from Donald, Helen and her son, there were also his sister, Hayley Bertrand, Jason Martins, Harriett Henderson, John Duncan, and brothers Jamie and Gary Monk.

He placed his hands on his head and could feel a headache coming on. Was it because of the stressful situation he was in? Or was he just dehydrated?

He rubbed the top of his scalp as he paced the earth, back and forth, mentally screaming at Grace to hurry up, but he suddenly stopped walking when his ears picked up a sound above him.

"Shit."

The sound was coming from his left side, so he went to the right of the ditch and looked up to get a better view of what was approaching. It was just a rustle of a branch, so it could have been a deer or a badger or ... something.

The noise had stopped and was then replaced by the sound of dragging feet. He had heard that sound before. The sound of clumsy feet could only mean an exhausted survivor or the dead.

Gavin remained gazing up, heart slamming his ribcage, and held his breath as the noise stopped. He released a long and slow breath out before taking in another gulp of air, and could hear the dragging sound once more. He had a knife on him, but he still didn't want to put one of the dead down if he could avoid it.

A face emerged above him. It was a dead face, and Gavin cursed and took out his knife. The creature shuffled a few more yards and then stopped once it reached the edge of the ditch. It looked down on Gavin and snarled like a creature from prehistoric times. Gavin had never heard anything like it before, and braced himself for an attack. The male was as rotten as anything Gavin had seen and must have turned during the early days of this catastrophe. Its skin was yellow, clothes tattered, and the left side of its skull was exposed, making the Canavar even more chilling to look at.

It took a step forwards and fell into the ditch with a clump. It was face down and it appeared that it had broken its right leg, but Gavin immediately went over and stuck his knife into the back of its head.

Once he pulled out his knife, he chuckled, "Well, that was easy enough."

More shuffling could be heard and Gavin walked backwards, now with his back against the ditch and waited for the other creature.

"No more, please. No more."

The next Canavar was a female. It approached the ditch and fell straight in, as if it didn't know it was there. Like the one before, he ran over and stuck his knife into the back of its head before it had time to get up. He pulled out the knife and cussed when the handle was all that he had in his hand. The blade remained in the skull and Gavin desperately tried to pull out the blade. More noises came from above and he began to panic, still trying to prise out the blade, but it was in too deep.

Gavin stood up, knowing that it was fruitless what he was doing, and prepared himself for a battle he hadn't experienced before. He knew what to do, but actually doing it was another thing. The only thing he could do was stick his fingers or thumbs in the eye sockets of the oncoming Canavar. He waited for the dead bastard and could see the male approaching.

All Gavin could do was watch it drop into the ditch and then go over and kick it in the head multiple times, and hope that would be enough. Shoving his fingers in the eye sockets was something he didn't want to do, not if he could help it.

His heart was in his mouth as the creature dropped into the ditch. He hesitated a little and ran over to the slumped body and frantically kicked the head of the dead being. He brought the heel of his boot down onto the skull, and his boot managed to go through, black diseased brain sticking to the heel. With his stomach doing somersaults, he wiped his boot on the tattered clothes of the dead man and cried out when an object from above floored him.

The adrenaline coursed through his veins and he quickly realised it was a Canavar that had fallen on him. Paranoid about being bitten, he pushed the thing off of him and scrambled away to the other side of the ditch. He stood up and could see that the dead being was already on his feet. Another two fell into the ditch, and Gavin wondered how many more there were. Was there a horde coming his way, or was that it?

"Jesus Christ!" he cried. "No more."

He took an intake of breath as the first fallen one made its way over. He knew he had to dispatch this one quickly before the other two got to their feet and advanced towards him.

It snarled and grabbed his shoulder. Gavin never hesitated and grabbed the Canavar's face and pushed his thumbs into its cold eye sockets. Something spewed out of the sockets as his thumbs went in further. He didn't know what it was, but it twisted his guts all the same. His thumbs were in as far as they could go, but the ghoul wasn't going down. Gavin didn't know why. Maybe his thumbs weren't long enough to penetrate the brain.

He could feel his thumbs pushing into something; maybe it wasn't far enough. He threw the being from side to side, eventually pulling his thumbs out and throwing it to the floor. He stamped on the thing's head a couple of times, as the other two made their way over, and didn't know if he had the energy to put them down. He was exhausted.

Trying to get his breath back, he front-kicked the Canavar on the left, knocking it over, and tried to put the other one down. As soon as they grabbed one another, Gavin knew he didn't have the strength to put it down. They continued to grapple and Gavin cried out as Canavar Number Two was back on its feet and heading over his way.

Somehow the dead being he was wrestling with overpowered him and they both fell to the floor, with Gavin underneath the Canavar. He grabbed the creature by the throat, to stop him from being bitten, and was certain that in a few minutes he was going to lose this battle, especially with the other one near.

His arms shook with weakness and the Canavar was now only inches away from tearing a chunk out of his face.

Gavin closed his eyes and was seconds from releasing his grip, but the sound of a heavy thud opened his eyes and he could see the advancing Canavar falling to the floor, and the one on top of him was dragged off and Donald Brownstone stabbing the thing through its temple. He pulled out the knife, wiped it on the Canavar, and put it away.

"Enjoy your walk, did you?" he laughed.

"Thank fuck you're here." Gavin smiled and remained on the floor. He couldn't get up because he was so exhausted.

"Right!" Donald looked up the ditch and called up. "Have you tied that rope around the tree?"

"Yes," Gavin heard a familiar voice shout. It was Grace.

"Good. Throw it down."

Gavin sat up and blue rope dropped into the ditch.

Donald smiled at Gavin. "You first. I might need to help you up, you dig what I'm sayin'? You look fucked."

CHAPTER TWELVE

Yoler and Dicko sat on the floor, listening to the dozens of hands slapping the outside of the cellar door, and both had their knees up with their heads lowered. There was nothing they could do. All they could do was wait, and hope that the dead eventually became distracted and went elsewhere.

Dicko couldn't see it happening.

He was quite happy to wait a while, but overall, he was convinced that they were putting off the inevitable. If they had any chance of getting out of the cellar, they would have to fight their way out.

For minutes, the door continued to be pounded, but the noise diminished until it sounded like there were only three or four behind the door. They still slapped against the door, but at least the noise was tolerable now.

"I think I'm getting a migraine," Yoler moaned. "That's all I pissing need."

Dicko flicked the lighter and lit up the cellar temporarily and asked her if she was okay.

"I'm okay," Yoler said. "Just need to ride it out."

"Would a head rub help?"

"Not really, no."

A silence enveloped the pair of them as the slapping continued, but it now sounded like it was just two Canavars behind the door.

"I was thinking about Donald," Yoler blurted out in a whisper.

"Oh?"

"Just thinking about what he went through, and what you went through... I'm not sure I would have coped."

"Donald lost his son *before* the apocalypse," Dicko said in a soft voice.

"I know." She nodded and said further, "But still..."

"You do cope," said Dicko. "I don't know how, but you do. Although I did lose it for a while."

"No wonder." Yoler cleared her throat and looked around in the darkness. She literally couldn't see a thing. "Did you manage to take care of your son, like we did with Imelda and Simes?"

"What do you mean? Put him to rest?"

Yoler nodded. She had no idea why as Dicko couldn't see her. "Yeah," she eventually said.

"I managed to bury my son," Dicko said with a quiver in his voice. "But not my wife and daughter."

"Why?" Yoler then immediately apologised and said, "Do you mind me asking? I know you mentioned it weeks ago when we were playing that daft truth game, but you never went into detail as such."

"I don't mind," said Dicko. He ran his hands over his face, released a groan and said, "I met up with a guy called Bentley Drummle. I don't know if he was some kind of criminal in the past, but he had a gun on him that he called Glen."

"What?"

"Yeah, I know. A bit weird." Dicko began to chuckle and continued with the story. "Anyway, this guy and his partner had a camp in the woods. He had been predicting this thing for months, apparently."

"A prepper?"

"I suppose so," Dicko said. "I was with my son at this camp, and I asked Bentley to take me to the supermarket where my wife had gone before the announcement was made. I knew which one it was, but didn't want to leave the house because I had Kyle."

"But you were at this guy's camp, so you did leave your house eventually. You mentioned leaving your house a while back, but never went into detail why."

"I did eventually, but that's another story why I had to leave." Dicko cleared his throat and added, "So, to cut a long story short, Bentley took me to this supermarket in his car and we found my wife and daughter in our Renault Clio. They had both reanimated."

"Shit, sorry about that, Dicky Boy."

"Bentley shot them, but we had to leave them there. I didn't mind. Those two sleeping together in the family car feels better than putting them in the cold ground, which is what I had to do for Kyle."

"And your son was killed in that camp?"

Dicko nodded. "Yeah, that was my fault. I let him go to the toilet on his own in the changing room. What I didn't know was that there was a Snatcher in the changing room."

"A what?"

"Sorry," Dicko laughed. "A Canavar. Anyway, he was buried at the camp that was called Sandy Lane. It was a nice service, to be fair, but sometimes the thought of him being stuck in that ground..."

Dicko allowed his sentence to linger and the two of them remained silent for a while. Dicko could hear an intake of breath and knew Yoler had more to say.

"So why did you leave your house in the first place?"

"I didn't want to." Dicko answered straightaway. "I wanted to stay there in case my wife and daughter came back, but we didn't have a choice in the matter." Dicko paused, but Yoler never persisted with more queries, as she knew that her male companion was ready to speak further.

Dicko said, "I had a neighbour called Daisy. Her husband and one of her daughters had turned, but we all kept quiet for a month or so. We got talking eventually and she and her other daughter, Lisa, stayed with me for a couple of days."

"Just a couple of days?"

Dicko could understand why Yoler was confused and decided to elaborate. Why not? They weren't going anywhere for a while.

"Our house, as well as others, was targeted by scavengers," Dicko explained. "A guy came in and went upstairs to where we were hiding. I hit him with a hammer and he fell and died. My first human kill, and it was an accident."

"And I take it these guys forced you to leave?"

"Well, they were a notorious family called the Murphys. They came into the house and we all hid. They found the body of this guy called Lance, their brother. They went in and searched the house. They found Daisy and her daughter."

"What happened then?"

"Well," Dicko released a depressed sigh when a flashback entered his mind. "To her credit, she never told them that Kyle and I were in the house."

"So they thought that your house was hers, and..."

"And they thought she was responsible for killing this Lance character," Dicko decided to finish off Yoler's sentence for her. "Kyle and I remained hiding in the cupboard as they were being dragged out of the house. The guilt I felt, and still feel, was quite overwhelming."

"You had a son to protect," Yoler jumped in. "If anything happened to you..."

"I know, but it doesn't stop the guilt."

"And the mother and daughter? What happened to them?"

"The father of this Murphy family caved Daisy's head in with the butt of a shotgun."

"Jesus Christ on a cross!"

"Tell me about it."

"And the daughter?"

"She was thrown into the back of a truck. She turned up at the Sandy Lane camp when a resident went out on a run and brought her back. Apparently, the same family that killed Daisy was responsible for killing his son years ago. The girl, as well as many others, eventually died when the camp was attacked by the dead."

"Jesus, and what—?"

Dicko shushed the woman and this made Yoler stop talking. Almost.

"What is it?" she asked.

"Can you hear that?"

"I can't hear fuck all."

"Exactly."

"Exactly?" She huffed. "What do you mean, exactly?"

"They must have gone elsewhere, probably to another part of the pub."

"So what do you want to do?"

"Grab your bag." Dicko flicked the lighter and the cellar lit up. He looked at Yoler's face and smiled. "Time to go."

CHAPTER THIRTEEN

Donald Brownstone trudged through the bracken with Grace and Gavin lagging behind. Donald and Gavin were exhausted and Donald felt a lie down in the darkness would be needed if he had to manage through the rest of the day. He looked over his shoulder and told the guys that they should be back at the camp in another five minutes or so.

"Donald, wait!" Grace called from behind.

Donald stopped and turned around. "What is it?" he puffed. He could see both Gavin and Grace had stopped walking, and both were looking to their right.

Donald looked in the same direction and released an angry huff, shaking his head with anger. Two male Canavars were slowly shuffling through the woods, twenty yards away, but hadn't spotted Donald and co yet.

"I'm ready to fall down," Gavin said. "I couldn't possibly put another one down."

"Stay there," Donald instructed the pair of them.

"Just leave them," Grace said in a whisper.

"No chance." Donald put his hands on his hips and gazed at the two dead, seething. He hated these things. "They're too near the camp, you dig what I'm sayin'? I'm not taking any chances."

He quickened his feet and moved in the direction of the dead. They spotted him and headed towards him. Donald pulled out his knife and assessed the situation. One was behind the other, so if he quickly put down the first one, he would have plenty of time to remove the second without putting himself in danger.

Donald rammed his blade into the side of its head, but it dropped quickly and he had no time to retrieve his blade as the second one grabbed him. He grabbed the hair of the Canavar and with what strength he had left, he smashed its head off of the nearest tree. He became a little over zealous and hit its head off the tree six times before allowing it to drop to the floor. He looked down, panting hard, and could see that he had smashed its diseased brain in. He made tired steps to the first body, bent down, and pulled out his knife, wiping the blade on the clothes of the deceased by his feet.

He stood up, hearing his knees crack, and looked over at Grace and Gavin who stood looking over, with wide eyes.

Donald smiled and made his way back over.

"No more," he moaned to himself. "I'm dead on my feet."

Once he was back with Gavin and Grace, he told them that he needed to sit down for a couple of minutes. His heart was beating out of his chest and thought that it'd be Sod's law that he had survived the apocalypse for nearly twelve months, only to die from a cardiac arrest.

Neither Gavin or Grace complained, and both stood patiently as Donald sat on the floor, against the tree.

"I hope that was just a one off," Grace said, looking around the area, seeing if there were any more lingering about.

"Me too," Donald spoke with a nod. "We can't just assume that it was, though."

Neither Gavin or Grace responded and waited for Donald to rise to his feet. Eventually he did. He put his arms in the air and stretched his back, making a groaning sound, before leading the way back to the camp once more.

Like two obedient dogs, Grace and Gavin followed behind.

CHAPTER FOURTEEN

"Ready?" Dicko asked in the darkness.

He received a positive reply from his female companion, and slid the bolt across and opened the cellar door by an inch. It took a while before his eyes could be accustomed to the light from inside the pub, and after twenty seconds had passed, he could see perfectly. From what he could see, it looked clear of danger. He couldn't hear any noises, so he opened the door wider and stuck his head out. He was certain that they were still in the establishment and had moved to the bar area, but the lounge area of the pub was clear.

Dicko turned to Yoler and announced that the area was clear, or at least that was what he thought. The main door was only yards from the cellar door, so escaping the place was an easy feat.

He left the door open and grabbed his bag off of the floor, and threw it over his shoulder. Yoler already had her full rucksack. He told her it was clear and he asked if she was ready.

"As ready as I'll ever be." Both straps were over her shoulder and she had her machete in both hands.

Dicko crept through the lounge area with Yoler closely behind, and both could see that the dead had gone into the bar area. They had no idea why this was the case, whether they had been distracted by a noise or something, but they were all there and this made Yoler and Dicko's escape easy.

"Where to now?" Yoler asked.

The pair of them were outside the pub, on the outskirts of the town, split on what to do next.

"Well, our bags are full," Dicko eventually spoke and looked to his right, down the road where the residential area was. "Maybe we should just head back. We can come back and search the houses tomorrow."

"I'm happy with that," she said. "We'll search for medical stuff as well as food."

She didn't specify why she needed medical accessories, and Dicko never asked. Yoler thought it'd be advantageous to have some kind of first aid kit, or even make up one with whatever she could come across. Most homes, in the old world, had some kind of medical gear. Whether it was just plasters, bandages, or drugs that could help with certain illnesses, she thought that these kind of medical supplies for the camp would come in handy.

Over the last few weeks, David had cut open his finger on a twig, which could have been taken care of with a plaster. Gavin had sprained his wrist two weeks ago when chopping wood. He had to rest it, but with the correct equipment it could have been strapped. And Helen had been suffering headaches over the last few days. It may have been dehydration related, but painkillers could have helped.

They strolled along the bendy country road and began to talk about Donald, and how he didn't seem to be as annoying compared to the first time they had met him.

When Brownstone was living with them at the farm, he was aggressive and argumentative, resulting in him being kicked out. Once the place was torched by Hando and they had to flee to the very same camp where Donald was staying, he seemed to have mellowed.

He still had his moments, but he was tolerable.

He could have been smug about them having to stay with him, especially after kicking him out, but he never dwelled on it. In truth, he was glad to have company again, especially Helen and David, two people he had grown close to during these crazy days.

Yoler slapped Dicko on the arm and the man stopped walking and screwed his face at her.

"What is it?" he asked.

"You were miles away," she snapped. "Humming some tune."

"I was humming a song by Radiohead."

"Yeah, well, you need to concentrate," she said. "I called your name a couple of times and no response."

"So?" Dicko hunched his shoulders. "What's the matter?"

"Can't you hear it?" Yoler groaned.

Dicko shook his head. "Hear what?"

"Listen." Yoler held up her finger and looked at her male companion.

Seconds passed and she could now tell by his face that he could also hear it. A vehicle was heading their way.

"In there." Dicko pointed into the woods and the pair of them crouched down once they were around ten feet in. They waited and the sound of the engine grew louder. The vehicle didn't seem to be in a rush and passed them by slowly, around twenty mph, and they could both see it was a large white Transit van.

They stood once the coast was clear and Yoler was the first to speak.

"What do you reckon?" she asked Dicko. "One of those meat wagons?"

Dicko puffed out his bottom lip, unsure what to think. "Not sure. I've been on the road for months and I'd never heard of these meat wagons up until a few days ago."

"Imagine it was true."

"Best not to." A shudder went down Dicko's vertebrae as he made his way back to the main road. They walked side by side and guessed another hour or so and they'd be back at the camp.

"I suppose it's not surprising that this kind of thing happens," Yoler began to speak. "It's been nearly a year since it kicked off. With the boats and planes that transport gas and food not running anymore, people still need to eat."

"True." Dicko nodded the once. "We just need to try and stay off the menu. It's not something that I've thought about, even when I was at my lowest ebb, months ago, and hadn't eaten in a week."

"You would never consider it?"

"I'd rather starve."

CHAPTER FIFTEEN

Grace, Gavin and Donald were minutes away from reaching the camp and no words were spoken from the moment they left the ditch, to where they were now. Gavin was carrying the rope that had saved his life, and Grace walked alongside him, close to tears, relieved that he was still alive.

Donald Brownstone walked with his knife in his clammy right hand, looking left and right as they progressed through the plantation. He wasn't taking any chances. A week ago he had a machete, but had lost it on a supply run. Two Canavars had burst out of a café kitchen door, where he and Gavin were, and he killed one by burying the blade deep in the dead being's head. The blade was stuck and he was finding it difficult to retrieve the weapon, which had to be left as more of the dead turned up. He and Gavin fled the area eventually, on foot.

On their travels, over the last three weeks or so, they had never come across a vehicle that was in working order. But even so, now dwelling in the camp, there wasn't really anywhere to park a vehicle. Unless they left it at the farm or the edge of the woods, near the burnt out Mazda, and just hoped nobody took it in their absence.

The knife was all he had now, and Yoler was the only one left that carried such a large blade.

"You two need to do me a favour," Donald spoke up.

Neither of his companions responded verbally. They just looked at him, waiting to hear what he had to say.

Donald added, "You can't mention that there're Canavars around here, you dig what I'm sayin'?"

Gavin knew why Donald wanted them to keep quiet, but Grace asked why.

"Because," Donald moaned, "I don't want Helen, David, and the rest knowing. I'll keep a lookout during the day, and we'll all be in the safety of the cabin on a night anyway. I don't wanna cause any more stress for these people."

"But Donald," Grace spoke, "What if some turn up and you're not there?"

"I'll let Yoler and Dicko know about it. That's it."

"I don't agree." Grace shook her head. "I can understand why you wanna do it, but this could turn out to be a bad idea."

"I'm sorry, Donald." Gavin looked to the side at Donald, but Donald never made eye contact. "I know you have feelings for Helen and David especially, but these kind of secrets can cause harm."

"So we give the woman and child sleepless nights, because you don't like the occasional white lie?" Donald huffed. "For fuck's sake."

"Most of us are having sleepless nights anyway," said Grace. "At least people will be extra vigilant if they know the truth."

Donald ground his teeth in anger and kept quiet. He could see their point, but was adamant that his idea was still for the best.

"And didn't Simon lie to his daughter," Gavin began, "and told her that the Canavars were all gone? That didn't work out, did it?"

"No, but her last days were probably a lot more relaxed than if he had told her the truth." Donald scratched at the back of his head and now looked to the side, at Gavin. "Anyway, you didn't even know Simon."

"No, but Dicko told me about that story."

"I suppose there's no point putting this to a vote?"

The three entered the camp and could see Yoler and Dicko were back. Helen and Lisa were chatting on the steps of the cabin, and Donald assumed correctly that David was inside.

Helen stood up and smiled. "You okay?" she asked Gavin. "Grace said you fell into a ditch. Did you break anything?"

Gavin shook his head and looked at Donald. The strange look was noticed by Helen and Lisa, and Lisa asked the returning residents what was wrong. Yoler and Dicko had now shown interest and now Donald had a little audience to make his announcement to.

"We're just gonna have to be a bit more vigilant from now on, you dig what I'm sayin'?"

"No," Lisa huffed and was concerned about the tone in Donald's voice. "We don't dig what you are saying. What do you mean?"

David was inside the cabin, so Donald decided to blurt it out before the little man stepped outside.

"There's Canavars in the woods," he said. "Gavin was attacked by a few, and I had to put some down."

"How many?" Yoler asked.

"No idea, but it shouldn't be a problem."

"Not a problem?" said Lisa. "And how do you work that one out?"

"If we stay focused through the day, we'll be fine. We sleep in the cabin anyway. Just have to make sure David doesn't go off on any adventures by himself."

"Okay." Yoler pulled her machete from her belt and Donald asked what the hell she was doing.

"I'm going Canavar hunting." She then turned to Dicko. "Fancy coming? Better to get them before they get here."

"This is not a bloody game," Donald snarled.

"I know." Yoler walked up to Donald and playfully patted his cheeks. "If there're too many out there, we won't be stupid and put ourselves at risk. But if there're strays out there, we may as well put them down before they get to the camp. Any kind of lapse of concentration or distraction with David here could turn disastrous. It would only take one of them. One bite. That was all that was needed to kill Imelda, and her bite wasn't even that severe."

Helen nodded frantically and told them that it was a good idea. She knew that a part of Yoler Sanders, and maybe even Dicko, enjoyed the killing of the dead, but if it meant keeping her son safe, she didn't care.

"Okay." Donald sighed, "Don't be too long. Want company?"

Dicko shook his head. "We'll be fine."

"Good," Donald snapped. "I'm knackered and Gavin needs a rest, too."

Dicko and Yoler waved cheerio to the residents, went into the woods, and were out of sight minutes later.

CHAPTER SIXTEEN

With their weapons clasped in their right hands, Yoler and Dicko trudged through the bracken. The plan was simple. The pair of them were to walk through the woods to the main road, checking to their side for any surprises. Once they reached the road, they were turning back. The woods went on for miles, occasionally separated by country roads, and Yoler and Dicko didn't see the point searching for miles. As long as the patch of woodland near their camp was clear, then that was good enough for them as far as safety was concerned. It may have to be a daily thing.

"You honestly think there'll be more of the dead in this area?" Yoler asked.

"Probably not." Dicko twisted his neck and looked from side to side. "But it gets us out of that cramped camp of ours."

"Are you wishing we were back at the farmhouse?"

"Of course." Dicko looked at his female companion. "The only trouble was that it made us a bit of a target. And if these meat wagon stories are true, then if we were still there, what's to say that these cannibals wouldn't have attacked us while we slept?"

"Personally, I think the stories are bullshit," Yoler grunted. "I'm not saying cannibalism isn't happening, I just don't believe there's an organised gang out there doing this kind of stuff on a regular basis."

"I hope you're right."

Yoler stopped walking and gasped when she spotted something move ahead of her on the floor.

"What's up?" Dicko could see the look on her face, but couldn't see anything around him or on the ground.

"I think..." She paused and scowled in confusion. "I think I saw a snake."

"Probably." Dicko nodded and seemed unconcerned. "Was that it?"

"I didn't think we had snakes in these parts."

"I think we have grass snakes and adders in this country."

Yoler shuddered and said, "I'm not a fan of snakes. That's the first time I've seen one."

"Well, next time you see one, give me a shout," Dicko said. "They're edible."

"Ugh." Yoler twisted her face. "Fuck that."

Dicko continued walking, and lagging behind, Yoler made careful steps through the plantation, paranoid about coming across more snakes.

Dicko nodded up ahead and said, "The trees are thinning out now. We'll get to the main road, sit on the grass for a bit and have a rest, then head back."

"I ain't sitting anywhere where there're snakes around."

"Probably just a grass snake or a smooth snake. They're not poisonous."

The two sets of feet had reached the main road and the two individuals stepped out of the greenery. Both were pleased to be out of the suffocating trees and feel the gentle wind lick their faces.

Dicko sat on the side of the road and pointed his toes upwards, stretching his hamstrings slightly. He began to take his boots off and allowed his feet to get some fresh air. One by one he took them off, and the smell of the stale socks he had been wearing for the last four days made his nose twitch. With the clothes getting washed at the pond regularly, there was no excuse for the smell. Maybe he'd wash them himself sometime today.

With the thought of snakes in her mind, Yoler decided to remain standing and paced the middle of the road, waiting for Dicko to finish his resting. She looked to her right and could see thirty yards up that the windy road bent to the left, but to her right the country road stretched for a quarter of a mile and eventually bent to the left. There were trees on either side of the road.

"Sit down," Dicko called over to her. "You pacing up and down is getting on my nerves."

"Just get on your feet and get back to the camp," she huffed impatiently. "You can rest in the cabin."

"Just give me a few more minutes."

Dicko leaned over and touched his toes. He then began to do something he hadn't done in a long while. He began to do some leg stretches, the same kind of stretches he used to do when he attended the gym. He stood up and leaned over, pushing his hands against a tree, with his back leg stretched, trying to stretch out his calf, and then swapped legs and did the same. He then placed the palm of his left hand on the tree and grabbed his right ankle with his right hand and pulled his own leg up to stretch his quad muscles.

After fifteen seconds he swapped legs and did the same procedure. Yoler was giggling at him, but he ignored her. Once he was done, he walked over to her and asked if she was ready.

"I was ready five minutes ago," she said. "Shame there're no Canavars. Could have done with a bit of excitement."

"I think I've had enough for one day."

Yoler's eyes narrowed and this was noticed straightaway by Dicko. She was looking to her left and he looked in the same direction, wondering what she was staring at.

A bearded man emerged from around the corner and had his head down. Neither Yoler or Dicko said a word. The man's clothes were dishevelled and he looked thin, too thin. He was twenty yards away from Yoler and Dicko, and he finally raised his head and stopped walking once his eyes clocked the two of them.

"Jesus Christ on a cross!" the female blasphemed, as she usually did. "Well, I don't pissing believe it. Look who it is."

Dicko could feel his rage building and wanted to run over to the man and stab him to death, but the man waved at the two of them, revealed a wide smile and pulled out two machetes that were strapped to his back.

It was Hando.

"I'm ready when you are," Hando laughed.

Yoler took a step forwards, but Dicko grabbed her by the arm and pulled her back.

"We can take him," she snapped.

"Maybe." Dicko nodded and didn't look too sure. "But even if we did kill him, we could sustain an injury in doing so."

"So?"

"A bad cut can become infected if we don't have the right meds for it. I know we're gonna check out the houses for medical stuff tomorrow, but that doesn't help us today. At worst, an amputation could kill you with the loss of blood."

"So we just leave him, eh?"

Dicko never answered and Hando called over, "I'm sorry for your friend," he said. "But to be fair you did kill two of mine."

"So your pal with the Chelsea top didn't make it?" Dicko was certain that one of Hando's henchmen that had lost his hand had died anyway from blood loss. What he didn't know was that it was Hando himself that had killed him.

"That's right, brother," said Hando with a chuckle. "I've been all on my lonesome since then. As you can see, I'm not in the best shape."

"My heart bleeds."

Hando smiled widely and could see that during the conversation the two hadn't pulled out their weapons. He put his back and eventually put the machetes back in the leather holsters that were strapped to his back.

"So now what happens?" Hando asked the two of them. Neither one could give the man an answer.

Yoler knew it wouldn't happen, but she said, "Now, you toss those blades over to us and give yourself up. We have some justice to serve you."

"So, you want to kill me because of that one weak guy?" Hando shook his head and yelled, "You did two of my guys!" This was a complete lie. Dirty Ian was killed, but Hando had killed Wazza himself.

"Maybe," she said. "But we have two women back at our camp that would love to stick a blade in you."

Hando looked confused and opened his mouth to speak, but nothing came out.

"Let me explain," Yoler began. "A while back, you and your scummy pals broke into a caravan where a woman and her two daughters were staying."

They could tell by Hando's face that he knew straightaway who she was talking about.

"Two daughters?" Hando looked to the side in thought.

"Yeah, the other one, the one that's with us, ran while you and your cronies raped Lisa and killed her fourteen-year-old daughter."

"Lisa. Is that her name?" Hando ran his fingers over his bald head and added, "I liked her. Even when she attacked me, I still liked her. Didn't realise that there was another present."

"You're one sick individual," Yoler snarled.

"We're all on borrowed time, sister. I'm just trying to survive and have as much fun as I can. That's all." Hando pointed ahead of them and said, "Now, I'm going that way, so I need to walk past you." He put his hands behind his head and patted the handles of the machetes. "Will I be needing these?"

"No." Dicko gently took Yoler's arm. "We're going."

"Good." Hando smiled. "Not in the mood for bloodshed."

Dicko walked into the woodland and dragged Yoler in with him. They walked, constantly looking over their shoulder, and could see Hando on the road, passing by them.

"Give my regards to Lisa." He chuckled and continued with his walk. He had now disappeared from their view and Yoler shrugged off Dicko who still had a hold of her.

She huffed, "We should have killed that fucker."

"It's not worth the risk," said Dicko. "We could get seriously injured, or worse."

"It just doesn't seem right to let him go like that."

"I know. We can handle ourselves, Yoler, but that guy's a maniac. Do me a favour."

"What?"

"Don't tell anyone about this," he said. "I don't think he'll be a threat, so no point making the camp paranoid. With these meat wagon stories, as well as the dead, it'd be just too much for some to take."

"If you say so."

"Trust your Uncle Dicko," he laughed.

"God, don't say things like that."

"Why not?"

"Because it's weird. We've slept together, remember?"

"Fair point."

CHAPTER SEVENTEEN

Helen Willis groaned as she stood to her feet and decided to go into the cabin and see if her son was okay. Lisa and Grace Newton had had a tearful heart to heart, and Gavin was sat up against a tree, exhausted by the ditch incident.

Helen left the door open as she stepped inside the cabin, to allow what little light there was outside to creep in, and could see that her little boy had dozed off in the bed.

"Bless him," she said with sadness in her words.

This wasn't right. Living in this hellish world was too much for a small child, especially a sensitive soul like David.

She sat at the side of the bed and looked at her special man. She stroked his forehead and her eyes dampened as he began to moan in his sleep. Was he having a bad dream? She could protect him in the outside world, but she was helpless when he was sleeping.

He threw his head to the side and Helen wondered if she should wake him up. David moaned, "No, no, no."

That was enough for Helen. She shook her little boy until his eyes opened. He looked confused, and began to look around the cabin. The disappointment on his face was clear, and for a while he must have thought that he was back in the old world, back in his old bedroom.

Looking around the cabin had made him realise that the reality was that he was living in a world where his friends were no more. His school days would never come back, there was no Xbox anymore, no football practice and no TV.

He sat up and said nothing to his mum, who was still stroking his head, and then burst into tears.

Mother and son hugged and Helen's heart broke for the umpteenth time for this little man that she had brought into the world, and she stayed where she was until he was finished. She loved David. He was everything to her, in fact he was all that she had left, but if she could get the time back, she never would have had him. This was no place for an adult, let alone a child. This was hell on Earth.

David had soaked his mum's shoulder and had finally stopped crying. They broke away from their embrace and Helen wiped his tears away with her thumb and kissed him on the head.

"My poor boy," she cried. "My poor sweet boy."

There was a knock on the cabin door and Helen and David looked over to see Donald standing just outside, on the top step.

He asked, "Everything okay?"

Helen and David nodded.

Despite not being invited in, Donald stepped inside and produced a wide smile when David looked at him.

"Alright, champ?" Donald bellowed and could see he was upset. "What's up?"

Helen stood up and Donald flashed her a wink, as if to say: 'I've got this.'

Helen walked by Donald and whispered to him that her boy had had a bad dream. She left the cabin with no protest from the wee man, and Donald took her place, sitting on the side of the bed.

"I hate nightmares, don't you?" Donald rubbed the top of David's head and began to have thoughts about his own son.

David nodded and wiped his eyes.

"The good thing about nightmares is that you can escape them and they sometimes don't come back."

David looked baffled by Donald's ramblings, but never said anything.

Donald could see David's confusion and explained in short, "What I mean is that you eventually wake up."

"Oh." David took in a deep breath and asked, "Donald?"

"What is it?"

"Where do they come from, the nightmares?"

"Jeez. Now *there's* a question." Donald was lost in thought and had no definitive answer. "I think most nightmares occur during the night, but you only had a nap. I suppose being anxious can make you have nightmares. And let's be honest, we're all anxious."

"Anxious?"

"It means when you're scared."

"Oh."

Donald put his arm around the boy that he had grown fond of over time, and gave him a kiss on the top of his head. He had never said anything to David, or Helen for that matter, but he loved the little fellow. He felt sorry for him, and from being a father himself he felt protective towards him.

"My worst dreams are not really the nightmares, although I do get my fair share." Donald cleared his throat and added, "Do you dig what I'm sayin'?"

David shook his head, making Donald chuckle.

"Nightmares are pretty bad," Donald began to explain. "But it's the nice dreams that I hate."

"What do you mean?" David was still confused.

"A few weeks ago, I had a dream that I was in the park with my son. He was about four years old in the dream, and we went on the swings, the slide, and some climbing web that was made of rope. Anyway, after that we went for ice cream and went home and watched a movie together."

"I would love a day like that," David said with sadness. "Just one."

"Well, this was a dream, and it was very realistic," said Donald. "But when you wake up and you're in this cabin with seven others, it hits you like a sledgehammer that life will never be the same again."

David's bottom lip was pushed out and he dropped his head.

"I'm sorry," Donald began to snicker. "I'm hardly cheering you up, am I? I'm just telling you like it is."

David reached out and placed his soft warm palm on top of Donald's hand, making the middle aged man feel emotional.

"I'm glad you're here, Donald." The little boy spoke with a quiver in his voice. "I feel safe when you're here."

Donald grunted, trying to remove the hardness in his throat and rubbed the boy's hair. "I'll see you outside," he said. "I'll be going to the pond after, if you wanna come?"

"No thanks." David swung his legs to the side and got off the bed. "I wanna stay near mum today."

"Okay, little man." Donald headed for the door and said, "'See you out there."

CHAPTER EIGHTEEN

He looked up to the perfect sky and cursed the sun that beat down on his exposed head. The only way of getting away from being burnt was to go into the woods, but he hated being in there. He had always preferred to be out in the open, walking the streets.

Hando had reached a small village and could see that this little place called Burnside had only six houses, three on either side of the main road. If he continued to walk, he would have been out of the place in five minutes. It was probably the smallest place he had ever been to. There were just the six houses; no pub, school or shop. He was starving, so checking out the places was a must. He had had no luck in the last few houses he had been in, but had to try. He couldn't remember the last time he had food. Four days ago? Maybe it was longer.

Hando could see that all the main doors of the houses were closed. There were no vehicles on the drives of the houses, and he guessed that the people had either fled or the vehicles were stolen over the months.

He approached the first house on the left and tried the main door. He was surprised when it opened and looked to see that it had been forced open. This made his heart sink, as he was convinced that the house had nothing of interest for him. He checked anyway.

He went through the kitchen and didn't even try the defunct fridge. The smell coming from it convinced him that there was nothing edible inside it. He decided to try the kitchen cupboards on his way out and now walked through the living room and went upstairs. The place smelt stale and desperately needed a window open, some fresh air.

He reached the landing and could see all the doors to the bedroom were open. There was no presence in any of them. The house was empty.

He released a sigh and went downstairs, ready to check the next place. He checked the kitchen cupboards but they were predictably bare. He slammed the last cupboard shut in anger and left the house. He stood outside the main door and closed his eyes, letting the wind caress his face. He had five more to check.

He went to the next one and the main door had also been forced open. Hando was beginning to think that this was the scenario for all the houses and that maybe a gang had come here a while back and checked out the places.

He went in, not expecting much, and the layout of the house was the same as the first one. As soon as Hando walked into the house he was in the kitchen. Like before, he left the cupboards alone for the time being and checked out upstairs. It wasn't just food and drink he was after; he was hoping for some kind of sports bag or rucksack. He didn't have anything to put in the bag, but it was only a matter of time.

Before his feet reached the landing, his nose screwed and his stomach twisted when he could smell death. He pulled his t-shirt up and over his nose, and went into the bedroom where he could hear the sound of flies buzzing.

He stepped inside and could see a man and a woman lying on the carpet, near their beds. They were both fully clothed, the corpses weren't that old. Their features were still visible and Hando guessed that the bodies were a few months old. It looked like the pair of them had been stabbed to death. Their bellies were covered in old blood and there were defensive marks on the hands of the woman.

Somebody had come in and killed them. The only reason the couple had been killed was for the supplies that they had left. It must have been, Hando thought. Why else would you kill two people months into the apocalypse?

He went downstairs and checked the kitchen cupboards before exiting the main door. They were also bare.

Hando shook his head and went to the next house. Any excitement that he had had now evaporated after what he had witnessed in the last two houses.

He tried the main door of the house, expecting this one to be open as well. It was, but this door hadn't been forced open. There wasn't a mark on the door, or at the side of it where the lock was.

Hando kept his blades on his back, but had a funny feeling about this house. He stepped into the kitchen and could see that the place was immaculate. There wasn't a sign of any dust or a left out dirty plate or cup.

He went into the living room and had a quick scan before taking the stairs to the next floor. His boots reached the landing and the man checked the bedrooms one by one. Hando's eyes clocked something in the corner of the room, and he could see a small bin that had an empty packet of crisps in it.

The bathroom was the last room to check and the malnourished man was going to check the kitchen cupboards before leaving the premises. He had three more houses to check after this one.

Something made him pause. He had no idea what it was, as he hadn't heard anything, but he remained where he was and looked up to see the hatch of an attic.

A small smile developed on his face and the man made his way downstairs with heavy feet, shut the door loudly as he went into the living room and then opened the main door and closed it again, but remained in the house. Hando then crept through the kitchen and into the living room and sat down on the sofa. His back was straight so that the blades didn't dig into him, and he rested his hands on his thighs and waited patiently.

A few minutes had passed and the man could hear gentle sounds, feet walking, above him. It sounded like the individual in the house, who must have been hiding in the attic, was now in the main bedroom.

Minutes had passed and gentle noises could be heard making their way down the stairs, to the ground floor.

Hando took in a breath and waited for the door to open. Once it did, a young and fresh face clocked Hando and gasped. The young man was a teenager. He was six feet in height, extremely thin with prominent cheekbones, and had short dark hair. There was very little facial hair present, and Hando put this down to his age.

"Don't worry, young brother," Hando laughed. "I'm not here to hurt you."

The young man, only seventeen, was reluctant to step inside.

"Let me ask you something, brother."

"What is it?" the nervous young man queried.

"Why leave your door open?" Hando asked the boy.

"To make strangers think that there's nothing and nobody here," the boy said.

"Clever." Hando nodded and managed a thin smile. "I like that."

"Obviously not clever enough."

"Hando." The bald man smiled and offered the boy his hand.

The boy stepped inside and walked over to Hando. He stared at his hand and shook it. "I'm Benny."

Benny sat in the chair opposite Hando, and looked to be nervous. He didn't seem to be carrying a weapon, which Hando thought was very brave or very stupid. He couldn't make up his mind.

"Tell me your story, young man." Hando smiled and waited patiently for a response from Benny.

"Well..." The teenager struggled to respond. He didn't know where to start.

Hando told Benny to relax and take his time.

"I suppose the day started the same as it did with everybody else," Benny began. "We heard the news and stayed indoors. In fact, we managed to stay indoors for months before my dad decided to go out for supplies. He never came back."

"I've noticed there're no cars on the drives."

"The people in four of the houses packed up their cars and left within the month."

"And your next door neighbours?"

Benny shifted in his seat uncomfortably, and his body language suggested to Hando that the boy might have known about the murdered couple in the other house.

"When it was just me and my mother, the man from next door came round and asked if we had anything for them. They had run out of food. We had a little left, but he became aggressive and they had a fight. He knocked my mum out with a single punch and took what we had left. He was too big and I was too scared to do anything."

"What a scumbag." Hando shook his head and added, "And that was your neighbour?"

Benny nodded. "We didn't really know them that well. All I know is that their two sons were living in London."

"So where's your mum now?"

Benny dropped his head, and Hando knew immediately that his answer was going to be a sad one. He said, predictably, "Dead."

"How?"

"That punch I was talking about..." Benny looked up and added, "She never got back up. He must have killed her, or the fall did."

"I'm sorry, brother."

Then Benny said something that Hando was not expecting. "After I buried my mum in the back garden," young Benny began, "I snuck round to their house with a knife and a crowbar. I forced the door open and was ready for them to come storming down the stairs, but nothing happened. They had slept through it."

"So you killed them both?"

Benny nodded. "I hit them over the head with the crowbar, stabbed them to death after it. They put up a bit of a fight and both were screaming and out of the bed, trying to grab me. I managed to put them down with a few more strikes and then stabbed them a few more times."

"Wow. That's pretty heavy shit for a young lad."

"Maybe." Benny hunched his shoulders. "Fuck 'em. That man killed my mum and stole our food, which I took back."

"Wow." Hando was still smiling and said, "Maybe you should go on the road and join me."

"I've been here since the first days," Benny said. "Not too sure about me going out."

"The shelter here is fantastic," Hando admitted. "But it's no good if you're starving to death. You have to earn your food these days. You have to find it, steal it, and sleep wherever you can."

"I'm okay." Benny felt a little patronised. "I've put the dead down before. I have been out there when looking for food."

"Let me ask you a question."

"What?"

"How much food have you got left?"

"I have plenty of water," Benny spoke defensively.

"Any fool can filter a jar of water from a stream or a pond. I'm talking about food."

"Not much." It took a while for Benny to answer, but when he did, he seemed embarrassed about the honest words that came out of his mouth. "Enough for another few days ... maybe." He rolled his eyes and then hunched his shoulders.

"I've got a proposition for you," said Hando.

"Oh?"

"You killed those two next door, so I know you'd survive out there. How old are you? Seventeen? You're mighty fearless for a seventeen-year-old."

"You're waffling, Hando," Benny said, and Hando admired the teenager's balls for the way he spoke to him. Wazza, Dirty Ian and Q would never have spoken to him in that way. "What is this proposal?"

"Let's go for a walk. Get some air."

CHAPTER NINETEEN

A large pan was sitting on the stove with the fire underneath. Grace was boiling water for hot beverages and the rest of it was going to be used as drinking water. Yoler, Dicko and Gavin were sitting around the small fire, whilst Helen, David and Lisa Newton were in the cabin. Donald was at the pond, getting more water to be brought back and filtered. They had soup earlier, but Gavin could have eaten another bowl. The stomachs of all four were grumbling and their lunch earlier just hadn't been enough.

Yoler looked around at the three faces and could see that they all looked glum and despondent. Nobody had spoken a word in minutes.

"We're gonna have to do something about this," Dicko moaned.

Yoler looked up. She didn't know what he was talking about, and going by the faces of Gavin and Grace, neither did they.

"About what?" Yoler asked him.

"I know we're alive, and I know we have it better than most that are still breathing, but we can do better than this."

Dicko had paused, but Yoler remained quiet. She knew he had more to say.

"Hiding in the woods, eating soup, and living next to a pond is great, but we're gonna have to take risks eventually."

"Um..." Gavin cleared his throat. "What do you mean?"

"Once the vegetables have run out, then what are we gonna do?"

Gavin hunched his shoulders. "Hunt deer?"

"When was the last time you saw a deer in these woods?" Dicko laughed. "And what would we hunt them with? Spears?"

Gavin couldn't give Dicko an answer.

"We need to find an abandoned supermarket or wholesalers, or something. But we also need wheels."

"So what are you proposing?" Grace asked.

"Well, I haven't said anything to Yoler yet." Dicko looked over to his female companion and gave her a thin smile. "But the thought I had was to go out there, on foot, and try and find somewhere like what I have described."

"Impossible." Gavin shook his head. "After nearly a year, there'll be nothing left."

"You'll be surprised. Don't forget that most of the people that have died, probably got killed in the first month."

"You don't know that for sure."

"Anyway," Dicko ignored Gavin's comment. "Yoler and I will walk out there, but we could be away for a few days. This is not something that we could do in a day. If we find somewhere, there're two options. Yoler and I could try and get a set of wheels and transport the food, bit by bit, here, and then carry the stuff a mile or so to our camp. Or ... we can simply move into a new place. We have enough people to guard it from others and we have to think about the winter, when nothing grows."

"Winter is ages away."

"It'll soon come round," Yoler chipped in. "There'll be no berries to pick, no vegetables to grow, and we'd be staying near a frozen pond for a good while, possibly."

"That's what I was thinking." Dicko nodded.

"I'm up for it, Dicky Boy. When are we going?"

"Tomorrow morning. First thing."

The water was now boiling in the pan and Gavin got to his feet. "Who's up for coffee? Still got some left from that warehouse I went to."

Everyone apart from Grace nodded.

Grace puffed out a breath and moaned, "I miss chocolate."

Yoler started to snigger and nodded. "So do I. I would love to have my iPhone for a week, get the internet back, listen to music. It's ironic. This situation we're in is perfect for those things, because of the boredom."

"What about missing family members?" Gavin asked.

"Well, that goes without saying," said Yoler. "I'm talking about materialistic and other things. Anyway," she looked over at Gavin, "let's get this coffee."

*

Donald Brownstone took his boots and socks off and walked into the water, careful not to stand on anything that would hurt or injure the soles of his feet. Carrying a yellow bucket in his left hand, he waded through the water for a few more yards and dipped the bucket once the water reached just underneath his knees.

Once the bucket was full, Donald turned and made his way back to the water's edge. He plonked the bucket down on the ground and sat on the floor. He picked his socks up and pulled them over his soaked feet and then reached for his boots. He stood up and looked over at the cluster of trees. For old times sake he decided to go to the farm, to see how the old place was and to relive some times from last month. He didn't care too much for Simon Washington, but he was upset by his daughter's death that had occurred around two months ago.

Donald left the bucket where he was and walked around the pond. He went into the cluster of trees and was out on the field. He looked up the hill from a distance and could see the burnt out farmhouse. He managed a smile and then his face dropped once a figure could be seen emerging from the side of the place, where the burnt out Mazda sat.

Donald couldn't quite make out if the figure was male or female and began to slowly walk across the field. He didn't want to bring another mouth to feed for the camp, but he was intrigued to see who it was. With the individual checking out the farmhouse, Donald came to the assumption that the person was looking for a place to stay, possibly food as well. The individual didn't look like they were carrying a bag.

Donald's eyes narrowed as he walked and could see that the figure was a man, but not just any man. The man in the distance turned and had spotted Donald. Donald recognised the man, despite the beard on his face, and could feel his blood boiling.

He felt his pocket to make sure it was there and could see the man laughing. Hando had recognised Donald and began to taunt the man by waving at him. Donald was in two minds whether to go up there or not. He took a few steps forwards, but stopped when another figure appeared.

A younger man showed up and stood next to Hando. The two males began to talk, looking in Donald's direction, and Brownstone decided that taking on two men was too risky. Way too risky.

He backtracked and disappeared through the cluster of trees. He hid behind one of the trees and gazed at the two figures. Donald was paranoid that the pair of them would try to follow him.

He didn't want Hando and his partner coming across the cabin. That would be a disaster. He looked for a few minutes and released a relieved sigh when the two males disappeared and had decided to leave the area.

Donald looked out for a few more minutes and was satisfied that they had no intention of following him, so he began to make his way back to the cabin, looking over his shoulder every few seconds.

CHAPTER TWENTY

Donald Brownstone returned to the area where he and the rest were staying. He was greeted by smiles from Grace, Gavin, Yoler and Dicko, and assumed correctly that the rest of them were in the cabin.

He placed the bucket of water on the floor and Yoler could see by his face that something was wrong.

"Sit down," she said to him. "Something's up. Tell us what's wrong."

Donald seemed reluctant and looked agitated. He looked over at the cabin and scratched his head.

"Helen and David are inside with Lisa," Yoler said. "Is there something you wanna share with all of us?"

"I don't know." He shook his head and sat down by the small fire, in-between Yoler and Dicko.

"Come on, Donnie Boy." Yoler nudged him playfully and said, "Spit it out."

"Okay." He released a breath out and began. "I went to the pond and, for whatever reason, I went to take a look at the farm. I looked at it from afar and saw Hando." He turned to Dicko and said, "He's back."

Dicko gulped and had a quick peep at Yoler, which was noticed by Donald straightaway.

"Shit," he snapped under his breath with his teeth clenched, aware that Helen and the boy weren't far away. "You two fucking knew?"

Dicko looked over at the cabin and then quietly told Donald that he and Yoler had seen and briefly spoken to him when they were out searching for more of the dead.

"Why didn't you tell me?" he snapped.

"The same reason you don't want Helen and David to know. We didn't want to upset the camp."

"He was with another person," said Donald.

"Another?" Dicko flashed Yoler a quick look. This was news to them. "He was on his own when we saw him."

"Yeah, well he has a little friend with him now." Donald sighed and added, "Better hope he doesn't come this way. I'll kill the fucker with my bare hands."

"Let's be cool," Yoler advised. "But I think we should let Helen and Lisa know."

Grace nodded in agreement. "That guy and his pals raped my mum and killed my sister. I don't think I could keep this information from her."

"Just make sure David doesn't know." Donald spoke in a hushed tone. "When Helen and David first got here, I lost count how many times that poor guy had wet himself during the night."

The cabin door slowly opened and Helen and Lisa Newton stepped out. Lisa was the first to walk down the steps and sat with the group. Helen's face looked glum and Donald asked about David. Helen told him that he was napping. She shut the cabin door behind her and went over to sit next to Lisa.

"You guys look very secretive," Helen said. She looked at Donald and asked him what was wrong.

Most of them dropped their heads, including Yoler and Dicko, leaving Donald to be the speaker.

"Come on," Lisa Newton huffed. "Out with it. Something's wrong. I know it."

Grace looked up and said to Donald Brownstone. "Just tell them, before David wakes up."

"Okay." Donald ran his fingers over his face. The anxiety was clear on his face. "But you're not gonna like it."

"Maybe that's true." Lisa folded her arms, waiting for Donald to speak further. "But speak anyway."

CHAPTER TWENTY-ONE

They had a rucksack each on their backs, but all that was in them were two jars of water each. Yoler and Dicko said their farewells to the group and made their way onto the main road. They decided to visit the village once again, check out the houses, and then go elsewhere to find something that could benefit the group.

Their walk to the village was quiet and they were in two minds whether to go at all because of Hando now being spotted twice, but Donald insisted that he could handle Hando on his own, if he really had to.

They reached the village and could see the pub that they were trapped in only the day before. They looked around and were thankful that there were no dead about, and began to walk by the pub and down the main road.

Dicko and Yoler had passed the small primary school and looked to the houses that were on their left.

"Maybe we should check out these places on the way back," Yoler suggested.

Dicko nodded. "We could do."

"I don't want to walk too far. We could end up getting lost."

"Well, if this takes longer than we think, then we'll have plenty of places to sleep." Dicko pointed at the houses to their left.

"And how do you know people aren't in there?"

"After nearly a year?" Dicko widened his eyes and asked Yoler, "Can you see a single car in this street?"

Yoler shook her head.

"So what does that tell you?"

"You don't have to be patronising, Dicky Boy." Yoler began to laugh and rested her left hand on top of the handle of her machete. "There could still be people inside ... or the dead that are trapped in their rooms."

They gazed at the houses as they continued their stroll. Predictably, the front lawns were overgrown, weeds covered the drives, and some windows were smashed, doors broken open, but a couple of houses looked to be untouched.

"Can't see a single body," Yoler murmured.

"Maybe somebody cleared up," Dicko said. "In my old camp, we used to have a habit of dragging bodies to the side of the road so that it didn't block our way, as well as others, whenever we needed to go out on runs."

"That was very thoughtful of you," Yoler mocked. "I bet you used to put the toilet seat down when you were with your wife, didn't you?"

"Cheeky bitch," Dicko laughed. "Anyway, you don't really see many vehicles these days, do you?"

"The petrol has to run out sooner or later."

They walked for a further ten minutes and were now out of the village and on another country road, but there were no trees to either side of them this time. Overgrown and neglected fields were at either side of them and they could see an abandoned tractor at the side of the road, further up.

"Ever been this way before?" Yoler asked her male companion.

Dicko shook his head and pointed up ahead, in the direction of the tractor. "Wanna check it out?"

"Why? Even if it was working, those things are too bloody slow anyway, and the noise... You'd end up with a herd of Canavars behind you if you drove that thing."

"I'll take that as a no then."

The country road bended to the left and once it was cleared, it straightened up and declined and they could see another small village in the distance. But what caught their eye was a white delivery van that looked to be abandoned.

"There won't be anything inside," Yoler said before Dicko could get his hopes up.

"You never know."

"I bet you a handjob there's nothing inside."

Dicko looked at Yoler and smiled. He held out his hand and she shook it. "Done."

They approached the van and could see it was a food delivery van from a big supermarket chain. The doors were shut, it was parked properly, and there was no sign of damage to the van.

Dicko went to the driver's side and had a look in. He gazed to the side and said to his female companion, "Take a look."

Yoler stood next to Dicko and looked into the vehicle. There were two Canavars in the van. Both driver and passenger still had their seatbelts on and Dicko couldn't work out what had happened. Had they both been bitten all those months ago and tried to flee in the van, only to pull over because they were both feeling unwell? It was hard to work out, but they were there and they must have turned in the early days as they were badly decomposed, but still moving.

Yoler left Dicko's side and tried to open the back of the van.

"It's locked," she said.

"And I know where the keys are." Dicko flashed Yoler a smile and pointed inside the van.

"Where?" She returned at Dicko's side and looked in.

The keys to the van were still in the ignition and they were both convinced that the key to the back of the van was attached to the chain.

"Even if there's nothing in the back," Dicko began and added, "we can still take it back to the camp, if there's fuel still left. Just need to get rid of those freaks first."

"Ready when you are." Yoler pulled out her machete and tried the door handle, expecting it to be locked, but both were surprised when it opened.

The door being opened alerted both rotten Canavars who wriggled and squirmed in their seats, reaching out to grab Yoler Sanders and tear her to bloody pieces. Dicko went round the other side and opened the passenger door, sticking his knife into the skull of the thing straightaway. Yoler rammed her large blade under the chin of the former driver, the blade going in deeply, and removed it, wiping the dark congealed blood on its worn work attire. Dicko leaned over his kill and unbuckled the seatbelt, and dragged the body out by its boots. Yoler did the same, then leaned in again and took the keys that were dangling from the ignition.

She shook the keys and looked across at Dicko, who was standing by the opened passenger door, trying to get his breath back, and said, "Gonna see if one of these keys are for the back. But first..." He studied the key twice and smiled when it was clear on the dial that the tank was half full. "Perfect. We have gas."

Dicko went round the back of the van to meet Yoler. She took the keys off Dicko and looked at the keyring that had five different keys on it and tried the lock. Two keys and two tries later, the van's doors clicked open and the two stared at one another, reluctant to open the doors.

"You want me...?" Dicko grabbed the handles and Yoler stood back with her machete drawn.

He pulled the doors open and jumped back half a yard, but his defensive behaviour wasn't needed.

The two looked on open mouthed and it took a few seconds for either of them to speak.

"This must be a dream," Dicko spoke with amazement in his tone.

"How is that actually possible?" said Yoler. "After all this time, how is it possible?"

"Who gives a fuck?" Dicko pulled his t-shirt over his face. The stench was from the rotten fruit and meat, but it was the sight of the tins that had made the pair of them smile. There were twelve pre-packed open boxes of groceries and other accessories, and tins could be seen in some of them.

"I'm gonna do a stock count," Dicko said. Yoler remained where she was as Dicko grabbed a few made up empty boxes that were sitting in the corner of the van.

Dicko put out four empty boxes and began taking tins out of the twelve boxes, leaving the rotten fruit where it was. It wasn't just tins, there were also bottles of soda and a smiled stretched over Dicko's face when his eyes clocked a bottle of Jamesons' whiskey.

"I don't think we'll need to stay overnight," Dicko said. "I'm guessing that it's early afternoon, but I think we should anyway."

"Why?" Yoler scoffed. "Because you want that handjob where there's nobody about?"

"Well, that as well," he began to snigger and held up the bottle of whiskey. "But I want to neck this, alone, in a place that is more secure than some cabin."

"Okay. We'll drive the van to one of the houses in that first village we passed and stay there. Be nice to have a night away from the camp and stay in an actual bed. I don't know why we can't just stay in one of the houses anyway."

"Because Donald is paranoid about the dead and other humans." Dicko cleared his throat and added, "I suppose what happened at the farmhouse kind of confirms that he has a point, but those woods are doing my head in."

"So what's the plan?" Yoler asked.

"We're taking these tins and bottles with us, throw out the boxes with the rotten stuff, get a house for the night, and enjoy ourselves for once. We'll just tell them that we had to search for a while before coming across the van."

"I can live with telling them that, Dicky Boy. Ready when you are."

CHAPTER TWENTY TWO

The van entered the village and Dicko informed Yoler that they were going to try and find a decent place to stay. When he said decent, he meant a place where there was no carnage. Just thinking about sleeping on a mattress for the first time in a while made the man smile, and he told Yoler that when they headed back the next day, they were going to throw a few mattresses in the back for the cabin.

They pulled along the desolate road and Dicko pointed at a house four doors down that he wanted to try. He didn't want to park the vehicle outside the house where they were staying, just in case they came across unwanted visitors.

"I'll check the house out," Dicko said. "If it's fine, we'll leave the van where it is and move the food inside in case someone breaks into it while we're asleep."

"Okay," was all that Yoler managed and threw her head back. She was getting tired.

He stepped out of the vehicle and went over to the second house from the end. He tried the door but it was closed, and then ran at it with his shoulder, easily forcing it open.

He rubbed his shoulder and smiled. "Well, that was easy enough."

He looked over at the van and waved at Yoler, pointing in the direction of the doorway, telling her that he was going in. He didn't get a response from the woman and just went in.

As soon as he walked in, he could see that the stairs to the first floor were in front of him. There was an alcove to his left and he could see it was the living room. It was an open plan ground floor, and he could see that the room was clear before stepping in. He stepped in with his trench knife in his hand and knew that there was a kitchen somewhere. The room smelt fusty and his nose twitched when a small hint of rotten fish could be detected. He was convinced the smell was coming from the kitchen, possibly the fridge, and he made slow careful steps to the dining table that was at the end of the room.

He popped his head around the right corner of the room and could see a small kitchen and a side door that led outside.

The smell seemed to have dissipated and Dicko opened the fridge to find nothing inside apart from garnishes like mint sauce, English mustard, and a jar of jalapenos. He shut the door and checked the cupboards. There were tins of peaches, beans, and soup. There were thirteen tins altogether. It wasn't a lot, but the tins were going in the back of the van on their way back to the camp.

It was time to check the upstairs.

The man in his forties made his way back through the living room and reached the first floor in seconds. He looked around the landing and could see that the doors were all closed, making the area very dusky and difficult to see, despite it being during the day. The smell he had detected earlier also seemed to have grown stronger since he arrived on the first floor, and Dicko was sure that it was death that he could smell. It was something he had smelt many times before.

He opened the furthest door to his left and could see it was a spare room. The bed was still made and there were no personal touches to the room. He only looked around for a minute and then checked the next room. He heard the sound of the buzzing flies before the door was opened and pinched his nose as he stepped inside.

Just by the wallpaper alone, it was clear that it was a child's room, and Dicko gasped when he clocked the cot in the far right corner of the wall. A small limb, an arm, was lying in the middle of the carpet and was covered in blue bottles and excited maggots. He took a few steps towards the cot and some flies dispersed at his presence, but most remained on the rest of the little corpse.

Dicko decided not to look in. He didn't see the point. He knew that a child had been devoured, and went through possibly a few seconds or even minutes of pain that no child should go through.

Killed in its own bedroom, Dicko thought.

He was convinced that the baby had been killed by its own parents, a scene he had seen many times when scavenging for food. He went to the next bedroom with his knife out, convinced that the baby's murderer or murderers was in there. Back on the landing, Dicko placed his ear against the door of the next room and could hear nothing. He pushed down the handle and pushed the door open. His face twisted as the smell of death hit him, and he looked down to see a dead man on the floor.

The man was covered in the usual foul insects and appeared to have no eyes, probably eaten away. His head had received some trauma and his cracked skull revealed some brain tissue. He had turned. He was convinced of it. The man had turned and had his head caved in and was put down. By the side of the man was a claw hammer and Dicko was certain that *that* was what put the man down. But who put him down?

The bathroom was next. It was the final room on the first floor to check.

Dicko took in a deep breath, convinced there was going to be something in there that wouldn't be pleasing on the eye. The child had been killed, the man of the house, he presumed, had probably turned and had his head bashed in, but who killed him? Because he had been in these scenarios before, Dicko guessed that the man had turned, attacked the child and then was executed by his partner, the mother of the child. He opened the door and looked in. It appeared he was right, and it looked like the mother couldn't live without her little boy.

Dicko's eyes began to soak and he released a depressing breath out.

The woman was in clothes, her face blue, and she lay with her head to the side, in dark brown water that was her own blood once upon a time. There was a Stanley blade on the side of the sink where she had cut herself, and her arms were in the dark water. Dicko didn't need to check if the woman had lacerations on her wrists. He knew she had cut herself, and was certain that the cuts were deep.

This woman was in control in her last few minutes. She knew what she was doing, and didn't want to be in this world anymore. The knife hadn't been dropped to the floor, it had been carefully placed on the sink which was impossible to reach if sitting in the bath.

Dicko had an image of the woman, standing up in the hot bath, cutting her wrists and then calmly placing the bloody blade on the side of the sink. She then must have simply lay down and went to sleep, never to wake up again.

He had seen enough. He closed the door behind him and made his way downstairs. He took his empty rucksack off of his shoulder and put the thirteen tins from the cupboard into his bag, then left the premises.

He walked over to the van and opened up the driver's side and placed his bag on the seat."

"Well?" Yoler asked.

"Yes, fine. You?"

"Har-de-fucking-har." She smiled and shook her head at her male companion. "Is the place liveable?"

"No," Dicko sighed. "There's a family in there. Been dead for months."

"Oh."

"There're thirteen tins in that bag. Gonna try the house at the end and then I'll let you know if it's clear."

"Well, hurry the piss up," she spoke with impatience. "I'm bored out of my tits sitting here."

"Back in a bit."

CHAPTER TWENTY-THREE

After the house was checked and the food moved into the place once it was established that it was clear, Yoler and Dicko sat on the dusty couch and groaned. Their feet were sore from all the walking and they sat in silence for a while, looking at the dusty fireplace and the mirror that hung above it.

"I wonder who used to live here," Yoler said whilst yawning, making the sentence almost unrecognisable to the human ears.

Dicko understood what she meant and said, "Probably an elderly couple."

"What makes you say that?"

Dicko hunched his shoulders. "The mirror has an antique look about it, the couch we're sitting on isn't that modern, and who has a working fireplace these days? Also, in the bedrooms there are no toys or posters on the wall—"

"Alright, alright," Yoler laughed. "Jesus Christ on a cross, Dicko. You're boring the piss out of me."

"You asked," he said with a smile.

Yoler rubbed her eyes and released another yawn. She looked to the side of her, on the floor, where her machete lay, and began to kick her boots off.

"Did you check the attic?" She asked the man slouched next to her.

He shook his head. "That's the only place I didn't check."

"What if there're bodies up there?"

"You'd probably be able to smell it. Anyway, even if there are dead bodies up there, it won't affect us. We're only here for the night."

Yoler leaned to the side and rested her head on Dicko's shoulder.

"What are you doing?" he asked her.

"I'm tired. Thought I'd have a nap. Any objections?"

"Well..." Dicko began to move, forcing Yoler to sit back up straight. He stood to his feet. "Before we do anything, we need to barricade that front door."

"Right, well you do that and I'll go for a sleep on one of the beds upstairs, and your handjob will have to wait."

"A bit early, ain't it?"

Yoler hunched her shoulders and also stood. "Trust me. I'll sleep right through to the morning. Haven't slept on a mattress for a while."

"You do that."

Yoler was on her way to the first floor and left Dicko alone.

Dicko looked around and decided to move the armchair against the main door. He looked around for something else, but couldn't see anything worth using. He looked at the armchair and then up at the front door. "Fuck it. That'll do."

He took the short walk to the kitchen and looked in the cupboards to see the tins he had put away. When he first checked the kitchen, the cupboards were bare. He opened a tin of beans, using the ring pull, and checked the drawers for cutlery. He pulled out a spoon and ate the cold beans from the tin. He threw the dirty spoon in the empty sink and put the tin into the pedal bin.

He began to think about the attic and the dead family he had seen in the other house. Was it the same situation in this place? he thought. Or had the family fled. There were no vehicles present in the street, apart from the van they had arrived in, and guessed, like most streets he had been to over the years, that over the months people had fled and vehicles may have also been stolen. Dicko had done it himself, months back.

A month after he had been taken away from Colwyn Place in Little Haywood, he spent three weeks on foot, scavenging.

He wasn't asked to leave, like he had told the group. The story was a little more complicated than that.

Dicko, real name Paul Dickson, had been staying at a camp and had become a loose cannon. People were complaining that his behaviour was becoming erratic and that he made most people feel uncomfortable, especially when he just disappeared and went for walks.

However, he wasn't asked to leave. He was taken away.

On one of his walks, Dicko had killed a few men when the street was attacked. One of the men was related to Drake, and when the man and his gang arrived at Colwyn to chat with a man called Pickle, Drake told the street that the street would never be attacked again. But in exchange for the street to be left alone, Drake wanted Paul Dickson. He wanted to take him back and kill him, as revenge for the people he had killed.

A few people didn't want to give Paul up, but everybody agreed it was for the best. Paul Dickson was making people uncomfortable and his departure would also make the street safer, so it was decided that Paul had to go away.

Paul, at the time, understood the decision and thanks to his friend Karen, he managed to escape when Drake and his men whisked him away. Dicko was given a strong laxative by Karen and messed himself in the back of Drake's car. He went out into the woods, under guard, and managed to free himself with a razor that had also been slipped into his pocket by Karen when they hugged, and managed to run away, to Drake's annoyance.

A small smile emerged on Dicko's lips as he thought about his old friends and suddenly snapped out of his daydreaming when he heard the rare sound of a vehicle approaching. He hoped that the vehicle would pass by, hopefully ignore the van that was parked up. He went over to the window and peered out. The vehicle soon appeared. It was a large white Transit van and it stopped adjacent to the van that Dicko and Yoler had been travelling in.

"Shit."

Dicko continued to watch as two males and a female got out of the van and began to inspect the stationary vehicle. All three walked around the place. Two were carrying knives and one of the males had a shotgun in his hands.

Dicko wasn't sure who these people were. Were they individuals that were loyal to Orson, a name they had heard over the past few months, or were they just three people out on their own?

The three began a discussion in the middle of the road. It was clear on their faces that they thought that the owner of the vehicle was staying in the street.

The three men began to approach the house that the van was opposite. Dicko wasn't sure what they wanted. Did they want the keys to the van so they could take it for themselves? He wasn't sure.

Dicko didn't know how long he had been standing at the window. He continued to watch and could see the three leaving the premises. They went to the next house and it appeared they were slowly making their way down to where he and Yoler were staying. He guessed, judging by the time it had taken them to check the first house, that they were around ten minutes away. Three more houses and they'd be under the same roof as him and Yoler.

A scream was heard and Dicko looked on with his heart beating faster and could see one of the men dragging out a woman. She tried to fight back, but was given a kick in her stomach for her troubles. Then the other male picked up her legs and instructed their female colleague to open up the back. She did as she was told and the female was thrown into the back like a piece of meat, and the doors were quickly closed and locked.

"Why the fuck are they taking her?" Dicko couldn't understand it. "*Where* are they taking her?"

The penny had dropped and Dicko shook his head. It was a meat wagon. It must be.

"Oh, fuck. This is not Orson's men. It's a meat wagon."

Dicko removed the armchair from the door. If they tried the house and the chair was in the way, then that would highlight that people were inside. He then ran upstairs and went to alert Yoler. In a few minutes, they were going to have visitors, whether they liked it or not.

Dicko crept upstairs and began to check the bedrooms. The first one he checked had Yoler in it and she was about to get her head down for some shuteye. Dicko had startled her. She was about to scold the man for frightening her, but he held up his hand, stopping her from speaking.

"Before you say *Jesus Christ on a cross, you scared the piss out of me*," he said in a hushed tone, "you better come with me. We need to hide somewhere."

"Hide?" Yoler rubbed her eyes and was perplexed by Dicko's ramblings. "What the piss are you talking about?"

"There are people outside," he began to explain, "that are minutes away from getting inside."

"Who?" She swung her legs to the side of the bed and looked for her boots. She remembered she had kicked them off downstairs. "Orson's men? That Hando guy?"

"I think it might be worse than that."

"Worse? How?"

"I think it might be one of those meat wagons we keep hearing about."

"I thought they came out on a night?"

"It's the evening now, and I saw them throw a woman into the back of the van. Why would they do that?"

"Shit. Okay." Yoler stood up and told her male companion to wait whilst she ran downstairs to get her boots.

When she returned, she had them on, but the laces were untied. She bent down to tie the laces and asked him what the plan was.

"To hide." He hunched his shoulders. "There's three of them, but one has a shotgun. It's not worth risking our necks."

"But what about the woman in the back of their van? Was she alive when they threw her in?"

Dicko nodded.

"We can't just leave her there."

"We can and we will," Dicko said. "We're going into the attic."

Yoler seemed to be taking forever to tie her laces, prompting Dicko to whistle sharply at her, telling her to hurry up.

"Don't you fucking whistle at me," she snapped. "I'm not a fucking sheepdog."

Yoler followed Dicko onto the landing and watched as he pulled the cord that was hanging down. It was pulled and the hatch opened. Dicko turned and could see Yoler shaking her head.

"What is it?" he asked her.

"If we go in there," she pointed up into the attic, "we're kind of trapped."

Dicko sighed. She was right. "Don't know what else to do."

"What's the first thing you do when you search a house?" she asked him.

"Um..."

Yoler decided to answer her own question. "You go to the kitchen and check the cupboards. We've put those tins in the cupboards. As soon as those guys check the downstairs out, they're gonna know that people are here."

They both gasped when they heard the door being tried.

Dicko quickly put the ladders back in the attic and both agreed to hide. Yoler went into the walk-in cupboard, in the very same bedroom she was about to have a nap in, and Dicko went into one of the spare rooms.

He spotted a clothes cupboard in the corner of the room. He went over to the cupboard and dragged it out of the corner. He could hear individuals on the ground floor and went into the corner, behind the cupboard, and grabbed the sides and 'walked it' backwards, almost back to its original position.

Dicko took in a deep breath. He had been in dangerous situations before, but he was still nervous.

CHAPTER TWENTY-FOUR

Dicko tried to control his breathing as the sound of feet began to make their way to the first floor. He heard voices and it sounded like all three were in the house.

"Fucking hell," he murmured.

If action had to be taken, the ideal scenario would be to disarm the gun bearer first, but it was hard to see who that was when stuck behind a cupboard. More voices were heard and he could hear the female telling the two males that she was going to check the bedrooms. It sounded like one male was having a piss and the other had pulled down the steps to the attic. Dicko could hear a presence in the room and held his breath. A few seconds later, it sounded like the presence had left.

A minute had passed and Dicko could hear more scuffling on the first floor, and hoped that Yoler was well hidden.

"Hey, you two, come here!" the female yelled at her colleagues.

As soon as those words were heard by Dicko's ears, he knew Yoler had been found.

"Oh, shit."

A couple of bangs were heard and Dicko gasped, wondering if they were roughing her up.

"Get off me!" Yoler screamed out. "Why have you got me pinned to the floor? I was doing no harm."

Dicko scrunched his face in thought and wondered if Yoler was shouting out that kind of information, telling Dicko what the situation was. She was being pinned down. Was this her telling Dicko to attack them? If she was being pinned down, then at least two of them were on their knees, holding down the woman. The group asked Yoler a few questions, but it didn't sound like they were beating her.

"Fuck it."

He grabbed the wardrobe and tried to walk the heavy furniture out about a foot so he could squeeze through the gap, and by the time he had managed that, he could hear movement on the landing.

"Let's get her in the back of the van," a male said. "We're gonna have to tie this feisty one up."

"Are we gonna go?" the female asked.

"No," the same male voice replied. "We have more houses to check and I'm not going back until we have at least five bodies. It'd be a waste of petrol."

"Right," a different male spoke up. "Let's get her downstairs."

Dicko crept along the bedroom and could see that two males had a hold of Yoler, one on each arm, and they were dragging her downstairs, with the female with curly ginger hair in front of them. The female looked to be holding Yoler's machete in one hand and the shotgun in the other, and was laughing as Yoler called the woman names as she was being held in a shoulder lock by the two men.

Dicko crept across the landing and went downstairs, following them. He was aware that the woman had the shotgun, but she had it in one hand and it would take a few seconds to drop the machete, aim, and then fire. With the female leading the way, they were almost at the bottom of the stairs, and Dicko drew his knife back and embedded it into the skull of the man to Yoler's left. He kicked the man's back, freeing the blade, and the dead man fell over and on top of the woman before anybody knew what was going on.

The man on the right was punched in the throat with Yoler's now free hand, and before she could do anything else, Dicko rammed the machete, like a spear, through the back of the man's neck. He removed the blade as the panic-stricken woman dropped Yoler's blade and struggled to get the shotgun ready, and then Dicko threw his knife at the woman as the other man tumbled to the bottom of the stairs. The blade caught her in the face. She released a cry, dropping the shotgun, and escaped through the front door with just a superficial cut to the left side of her face.

She ran out into the road and fell over. She struggled to get back up, and once she did, she headed for the van she arrived in.

Yoler picked up the shotgun from the bottom of the stairs and went outside. She was in no hurry. She strolled along the road, holding the shotgun with two hands, and could see the woman trying the doors to the van and then checking her pockets. Yoler smiled as it seemed apparent that the keys to the van were in the pockets of one of the dead men.

Once it was clear that the woman wasn't getting in the van, Yoler raised the gun at the woman's legs and pulled the trigger. The ginger woman fell to the floor. She screamed out and placed the palms of her hands on her thighs, and called Yoler a fucking bitch.

Confident that the woman was going nowhere, Yoler could see Dicko exiting the house and asked him to get the keys to the van.

He held his hand and shook the keys. "Already got 'em."

Before Yoler could ask him to open the back to let the captured woman out, he began to unlock the van. He opened the shutter door and the short scream of a woman was heard.

"It's okay," Dicko said to the woman. He held out his hand. "Come on."

Now Yoler was standing next to him, but this didn't make the woman relax. Both could see that the interior of the van had old bloodstains on the floor and up the sides, and it stunk terribly.

"We saw those people throw you in the back of here," Yoler said. "Come on. Go back to your home."

The woman seemed less hesitant and thanked the pair of them as she climbed down. She then looked over to her house and ran over to the main door. Dicko peered at the injured woman by the passenger side. She was writhing on the floor, both legs bleeding, and Dicko felt no sympathy for the woman with the curly ginger hair.

"What about her?" Dicko asked.

Still holding the gun with both hands, Yoler said, "I've got some questions that need answering."

"Fine."

Dicko went to the driver's side and opened the door. He placed the key in the ignition and gave it a gentle twist. He stared at the fuel gauge and could see the vehicle was in the red.

He took the key out, went around the front of the vehicle, and met up with Yoler. The injured woman was a foot away, still moaning, and Yoler had the gun pointing at her head.

"The van's in the red," Dicko announced to his female companion. "So it's not worth taking."

"Okay." Yoler nodded. "I've got a few questions to ask Ginge here."

"Well, hurry up," said Dicko and began to yawn. "I wanna go to sleep soon."

Yoler opened up the old style shotgun and could see there were two barrels and one cartridge left. She snapped the gun shut and asked the injured woman her first question.

"What were you going to do to that woman? Why take her?"

The ginger hair woman laughed and spat on Yoler's boots. Dicko could see she was an individual in her forties, ugly, and her teeth needed serious work.

Yoler persisted, "Where are you based? Where's your camp?"

"Not far from here," she said, and then looked Yoler up and down. "Wanna join? I'd love to find out what your thighs taste like."

Yoler swallowed her anger and asked another question. "Is this a meat wagon?"

"I don't know what that means."

"Are you cannibals? Are you—?"

"We're not animals, love. We're just trying to survive." The ginger haired woman winced with pain and said with gritted teeth, "Once upon a time you and I probably had a family, passed each other on the street. I may have stolen your car parking space, ran on a treadmill next to you at the gym. Shit, I may even have served you at the restaurant my husband and I used to own, but times are different now. My kids are dead, my husband and friends are dead, and—"

Dicko jumped when Yoler pulled the trigger and the gun went off. The ginger haired woman's chest took the hit and she died immediately.

Dicko turned and looked at Yoler, holding the smoking gun, as if she was in trouble, and said, "I was actually quite interested in what she had to say."

"I wasn't. She was boring me." Yoler huffed. "Let's get her in the back of the van. I'll give you a hand with Laurel and Hardy in the house." Yoler looked at the shotgun. "May as well put this in with them."

"Okay." Dicko nodded in agreement. "Once we've done that, I'll drive the van to the end of the road and into the field, just in case more come looking and spot it."

"Okay." Yoler blew out her cheeks and said, "Let's get it done. And then tomorrow we go to the wholesalers, before going back to Donnie and the rest of the crew."

CHAPTER TWENTY-FIVE

Next Day

Donald Brownstone woke up and immediately got to his feet. He stretched his back and groaned with the pain. Sleeping on the floor was killing him. He decided that the best way to get rid of the smarting was to move. He crept through the dusky cabin and gently opened the door, then stepped out and winced when the daylight assaulted his sensitive eyes. Once his vision was restored, he could see young Grace, with her back to the cabin, building a fire with wood she had collected.

"Morning," Donald called over.

She turned around and smiled.

"Bit early for that, isn't it?" Donald grinned and added, "We're not doing breakfast anymore. Just lunch and dinner, you dig what I'm sayin'?"

"I know." Grace shrugged her shoulders. "I was bored. I couldn't sleep."

Donald stepped down to the ground and had a look at what she had built. He looked at the woman and gave off a thin smile. The poor thing had gone through so much. She had lost her dad, her younger sister had been killed, and her mother had been raped by a gang of mercenaries. At least they eventually found each other again.

"Be back in a bit," he said to the girl.

Before he took one step forwards, she spoke up. "Where are you going?"

"I set out some snares, six in all, so I'm going to check what we've caught."

"Rabbit?"

"Well ... hopefully," Donald laughed. "But it might be grey squirrel soup for lunch and dinner."

"Never tried squirrel," Grace said.

"The meat's tough, but it's edible."

Grace folded her arms and seemed unsure what to say to the big man she barely knew. Donald wasn't a man that normally engaged in small talk.

"Yoler and Paul aren't back yet," she said.

"I know." Donald smiled. "I don't think he likes being called Paul. Best to call him Dicko."

"You don't seem too bothered."

"I'm not. They can handle themselves. Hopefully this will be the last time, for a while, that we'll be missing breakfast. Depends on what they bring back."

"*If* they come back." Grace didn't share Donald's confidence.

"Oh, they'll be back." Donald clapped his hands together and huffed, "Right. I better go and check those snares."

"Can I come with you?" There was almost pleading in her voice. They were alive, but the boredom was contaminating their minds.

Selfishly, Donald wanted to be on his own. He knew he had a whole day with the group, and that thought alone depressed him.

"I'd be better on my own," he said. He felt terrible for the young girl, but alone time was needed for Brownstone. "Anyway, if your mum wakes up and sees that you're not here, she'll freak."

"Okay."

"Laters, kiddo."

Donald walked into the trees and had a rough idea where the four snares were. If Yoler and Dicko came back empty handed, the whole area of the woods would have to be littered with snares. The pond near the camp was a Godsend, but they still needed to eat.

Donald reached the first snare and sighed that it hadn't been touched. He released another groan and went to snare number two.

Snare number two delivered better results. A dead hare had been caught, albeit a skinny one. Donald untied the dead animal and reset the trap. He held it up and shook his head. The hare alone wasn't enough to fill him up. He pulled out a carrier bag from his pocket and placed the animal in. He walked a few yards north and then stopped. He had forgotten where he had placed snare number three.

He snickered at himself and groaned, "Donald, you fucking idiot."

He then looked ahead and saw a bush.

"Ten yards left of the bush," he murmured. "Of course."

He finally found the third snare and placed his hands on his hips like a petulant child. "Give me a break."

There had been no luck with the third snare and Donald wasn't confident as he headed for the fourth and final one.

"If it's like this now, fuck knows what the winter's gonna be like."

The man could hear a noise and became stealthier with his feet, picking them up as he progressed through the bracken.

He could see the tail of an animal near where he had set up the snare, and moved a few more steps to see a Golden Retriever digging in to Donald's catch. He couldn't make out what the animal used to be. He guessed a squirrel, but with its guts out and the dog devouring half of it anyway, the animal was beyond salvaging.

The Golden Retriever turned and snarled. It was very unlike a Golden Retriever's nature to be so aggressive, but things were different. This dog was starving, and nobody was going to take it off of him.

Donald shook his head and decided to allow the dog to eat his catch. There was nothing more he could do now. He walked backwards, keeping an eye on the canine. He guessed that it was probably a domestic pet a year ago, judging by the collar it was wearing, and he was surprised as it continued to gnash and snarl and slowly progressed forwards, following Donald.

"Don't make me do this, Fido." Donald pulled out his blade. "I had a dog like you when I was a boy. This ain't gonna be easy."

The dog continued to go forwards and a few steps later, Donald's heel caught an exposed tree root. He tumbled over and the dog attacked Donald, seeing his predicament as a sign to attack.

The dog went for Donald and the burly man held out his forearm horizontally to protect himself. The dog's teeth were felt through Donald's fabric, but before the Golden Retriever could sink its teeth into Donald's flesh, he rammed his blade into the side of the canine's neck and twisted the knife as the animal yelled and whimpered.

He threw the dog off of him before it bled out onto his clothes, and quickly got to his feet. Donald brushed himself down and looked at the animal he had destroyed. He didn't blame the dog. It wanted to survive and saw Donald as a threat to its meal that it was devouring, or even Donald as a meal himself. Attacking a large man like Donald was an ambitious attempt on the canine's part, but starvation led to desperation.

"Sorry, pooch," Donald released a sad sigh and looked at the dead dog on the floor and the rabbit in his bag.

"Fuck it. Looks like it's Retriever soup today."

Donald bent down, pulled the dog's head back by its ears, and dragged his blade across its throat. He crouched for a couple of minutes and watched as its throat bled all over the grass.

He then lifted the dog, and carried it as its throat bled out onto the ground, but not as profusely as before. He made his way back to the camp. The dog was going to have to get stripped and gutted before young David woke up. The little man was never going to touch lunch and dinner if he found out that dog meat was in it.

CHAPTER TWENTY-SIX

Dicko was the first to wake and sat up immediately, making his back cry out in pain. He rubbed his lower back on the left, and swung his legs around so his feet were now touching the floor. He had spent the night on the couch and Yoler was in one of the bedrooms.

He stood up straight and stretched like he used to when he used to attend the gym.

The gym. He smiled.

It seemed like a lifetime ago now.

When the apocalypse was in its infancy, Dicko was trapped in his home with his son and couldn't go anywhere for two reasons. His wife had taken the family car on the Saturday, the day the disaster was officially announced, to go shopping with their daughter.

The other quandary that Paul Dickson had was that they could have left, but his fear was that his wife and daughter might have returned to an empty house. They never came back.

He sat down on the couch and leaned back, thinking about the days when he used to work, go to the gym, and be with his family. He would give his life up for one more simple day like that.

He thought back to when he had to return to the gym, to get water. His neighbour looked after his son, Kyle, while he went out and he turned up at his regular place and had to break in. He remembered going into the dark reception area and being frightened to death. He entered the gym and saw a regular that he recognised had turned into a Canavar, or as some people called them from his area, a Moaner, Lurker or Snatcher. Some of the Colwyn Place residents from Little Haywood called them Creepers. He was taken by surprise by two of the dead in the gym. Back in the normal world they were fitness instructors, and Dicko had to remove them. They were his first kills.

His reminiscing was interrupted when he heard the sound of footsteps coming from above him in one of the bedrooms.

"Jesus, Yoler," he sniggered to himself. "You're like a rhino."

The feet of Yoler Sanders made their way to the ground floor, and Dicko greeted her with a smile when she walked through the door to the living room.

They both greeted each other with a 'good morning' and the female sat next to her male companion and released a breath out, resting her large blade on her lap.

"Christ." Dicko put his hand over his mouth and nose. "Your breath stinks."

"Cheeky bastard." Yoler took a peep at Dicko and added, "Yours ain't so good either. Smells like a cat has shat in your mouth."

"Alright." Dicko smiled at her predictable defensive response. "Calm down, woman."

"There're toothbrushes upstairs. We can use them."

The two of them sat in silence and gazed at the clock on the fireplace. It had stopped working, and the hands stated that it had ceased working at 2.34. Whether it was am or pm, neither knew.

"I wonder how many survivors are left," Yoler mumbled to herself.

"That's funny," Dicko responded. "I was just wondering how many Canavars were left."

"Do you think there're more Canavars than people left in the UK?"

"I have no idea."

"It's a funny name, isn't it?" Yoler said.

"What? Canavars?" Paul rubbed his hairy chin and queried, "I heard it was some professor that coined the phrase."

"He mentioned it on some of his interviews when he was on the news, when this thing had just started."

"I don't remember seeing him. I must have had a different channel on."

Yoler nodded. "He was Turkish, I think. He was an expert in biological sciences from Edinburgh University. Canavars is Turkish for monsters."

"Speaking of which." Dicko pointed at the curtains of the living room. There was a foot gap between the curtains and he saw a body walking by. He was convinced it was a Canavar and went over to the window to have a look. He saw it stumble away, but it wasn't the lone Canavar that concerned him, it was the two men that were checking out their van.

He continued to watch and saw the two men, both carrying bats, put the dead creature down. They dragged it to the side of the road and then continued to check out the delivery van, checking the doors.

Dicko went over to the arm of the chair and picked up his machete.

"Something wrong?" Yoler asked him.

"Not sure yet." Dicko put his boots on and said, "Going outside for a chat."

Yoler looked out of the front window and announced that she was going with him.

The two stepped outdoors, machetes in hand, and approached the men that noticed them seconds after they had left.

"Can we help you, gentlemen?" Dicko asked them.

"Alright, mate?" The one on the left was the first to speak up and pointed to the van. "Is that yours?"

"Sure is."

"Oh, sorry man." The man on the left was dressed in black clothes. "We were wondering who it belonged to."

"We're gonna be on our way soon."

The man on the right had a full grey beard, was tall, and looked menacing, yet his manner was kind when he opened his mouth.

"We live in this street," he said. "We're just making sure that everything is okay. We went to bed last night and woke up to find two vans in the street, so we're a little concerned."

"So you didn't happen to hear a woman scream, any of the vans pull up, or any kind of shooting?"

The two men looked at each other and looked embarrassed.

The man on the left spoke and said, "We were out on a run last night. Didn't get back till late."

"A bit risky," Yoler spoke up.

"It was. Took longer than we thought, but we ran into a bit of trouble."

"So you don't know about the woman from over there?" Dicko pointed over at the house. It was number thirty four.

"Brenda?" the man with the grey beard said. "What happened to her?"

"Know her?" Dicko asked the men.

They both nodded and the man on the left took over. "There's a few of us left. We're all looking after one another."

The man with the grey beard left them and went over to Brenda's house and knocked on the door. The woman opened it and the two began to converse.

"Most of us died," the man continued. "Including my wife. But we stuck together, buried the dead, and have been going on runs and growing our own produce since this shit began."

The man with the grey beard walked back over and Brenda remained by the door, waving at Dicko. He smiled and waved back.

The grey bearded man stood next to his companion and said with a smile, "These guys saved Brenda's life. Three people turned up and threw her in the back of that other van." The man pointed to the Transit van that was parked yards down from Dicko and Yoler's van. "They killed the three and let Brenda go."

"Where are these ... people?" The man on the left, dressed in black, asked.

Dicko answered, "In the back of that van. Ever heard of the meat wagons?"

Both men nodded.

"There's three people in the back of that van less to worry about." Dicko tossed a set of keys at the grey bearded man, which he caught, and added, "The van's in the red, but it could go for a fair few miles before it conks out."

Dicko turned and walked away from the two men, and Yoler followed.

"Thanks."

Dicko waved at the men and continued walking.

He and Yoler had to be somewhere.

CHAPTER TWENTY-SEVEN

Donald Brownstone exited the cabin and was carrying an empty bucket. Grace and Gavin were preparing the soup with the little water and veg they had left, and Grace's mother was going through the two times table with little David. Helen was sitting on the steps of the cabin and smiled as she watched her son and the woman talking and laughing. She could see Donald was about to go through the wooded area and head to the pond, so she asked if she could tag along.

"Sure," he said, and couldn't help but smile. "I'll be glad of the company, you dig what I'm sayin'?"

Helen Willis told her son that she was going to the pond with Donald. He acknowledged her with a nod, almost annoyed that she had interrupted his chatter with Grace's mum, and continued to talk with the fun woman.

Helen laughed and walked over to Donald and the pair of them walked through the plantation. A couple of minutes later and their short walk led them to the pond.

"Let's milk it for a bit," Helen said to Donald. "Being stuck in that place can be detrimental to your mental health."

"Tell me about it," Donald chuckled. "Any time I get a chance to go, I do."

"I've noticed." Helen pointed over to the other side of the pond and said, "Let's get the water from over there."

"Okay. Is that your way of killing time?"

"Kind of, but to be honest I wanted to have a look at the farm, just for old time's sake."

"I'll get the water first." Donald smiled at the woman.

He took his boots and socks off, and walked into the pond, careful where he was treading, and dipped the bucket until it was full. He headed back to land and put his socks back on his wet feet and the boots were next. He looked over to Helen and left the bucket where it was.

"Come on then." Donald used his head to motion Helen to follow him. They walked through the cluster of trees and stepped out onto familiar territory. They stopped when they were at the overgrown field, and looked across and up the hill where the farmhouse was. It didn't look too damaged, but Helen was aware that inside it was unliveable. She released a thin smile and thought of Simon and Imelda Washington. She wasn't a religious person, but she hoped that the pair of them were together, somewhere, and Simon was reunited with his wife and his son, Tyler.

"You okay?" Donald could see the sadness in her face and was unsure whether to comfort her or not. She didn't have tears, but he pitied the woman all the same.

"You want to go up there?" he asked Helen. "Have a look around?"

She shook her head. "No. I think I'd break down if I went up."

Donald bit the bullet and put his arm around the woman that he secretly loved. "You liked Simon, didn't you?"

She shrugged her shoulders. "It was good to meet somebody new, of similar age. I think, in time, we could have become an item."

"Oh?" Donald was hurt by Helen's confession. Was he invisible? Maybe she just saw him as a friend. Maybe not even that. Just a camp companion?

Feeling ridiculous, Donald removed his arm from around Helen's shoulder as she continued to speak.

"Simon and I had a lot in common," she said. "We had both lost our partners, we have a child each..."

"Don't forget that he was a cheater," Donald snapped.

"What?" Helen looked confused and took a look to her side, at Donald.

"Remember?" Donald looked flustered and added, "He told us as Imelda lay dead. He told us that he was a shitty husband and that he cheated on his wife, and—"

"Why are you bringing that up?" Helen took a step away from Donald and scrunched her face. "I don't get it. Why are you slagging off the dead?"

Donald Brownstone bit his bottom lip and looked annoyed. He stepped away from Helen and rubbed his head. He shook it and turned around, glaring at the woman he had fallen for months ago.

"Donald?"

"What's wrong with me?" Donald clenched his fists together and couldn't help himself. "I worship the ground you walk on, love David to bits, and you ignore me."

"Donald? What are you talking about?"

"I love you, you stupid woman! You go on about how you could have been with Simon, how you're lonely ... and yet you ignore me."

"I don't ignore you." Helen shook her head, baffled at Donald's behaviour. "Donald, I don't know what you're talking about."

"What's wrong with me? Why can't you be with *me*?"

"Donald, I don't know what to say." The penny had finally dropped with Helen. "I'm sorry. I don't see you in that way."

"Why not?" Donald stepped towards Helen and grabbed her arms with each of his hands. "I love you and David. I'd be good to you. I'd make you happy."

"Happy?" Helen shook her head and laughed. "I'll never be happy again. Nobody and nothing is going to make me happy again. Have you seen where we live? What kind of world we live in now?"

"We're better off than most folk. Give me a try." Donald kept a hold of Helen. "You won't regret it."

"You don't love me, Donald. This is about your cock, isn't it?"

"It's deeper than that."

"Donald," Helen groaned. "You're starting to hurt me. Let me go."

"Just fucking listen to what I have to say!" the man snarled.

"Donald, you're scaring me." There were tears in Helen's eyes and she was frightened. "Let me go."

"You need to understand." Donald gripped tighter, making Helen wince with pain. "I'd take care of you. Both of you."

"Donald. I..."

"You need to understand—"

"Let me go, Donald."

"Listen to me."

Helen kicked Donald as hard as she could in the shin, and the big man cried out and let the woman go. She turned around and ran away from Brownstone, into the trees, heading back to the camp.

Donald bent over and rubbed his shin. He then looked up and saw the back of her disappearing through the trees. "Helen! Helen!"

Donald refused to run after her. She looked frightened as it was and he didn't want to make anything worse, if that at all was possible.

"Fuck!"

With his adrenaline waning, he slowly realised that his behaviour was unacceptable. He smacked the palms of his hands off his head in frustration, and began to cuss and call himself names whilst pacing back and forth.

He couldn't go back to the camp how. Not yet. It was too soon. After the way he had behaved, Helen probably wouldn't want him in the same room, so sleeping in the cabin was out of the question. The people of the camp would pick up on the negative vibes between Helen and Donald and would ask questions, especially Yoler.

"Donald, you fucking idiot."

He walked through the cluster of trees and reached the pond. Helen was nowhere to be seen and the bucket of water was still sitting on the ground. He patted his pocket to make sure his knife was still there, puffed out a breath, and went back through the trees and into the overgrown field.

Donald was walking with angry steps and was heading to the hill, to the farmhouse. He had some stress to walk off. He didn't know where his walk was going to take him, but he couldn't go back to the camp. He would rather be out in the open with the Canavars than be in the presence of Helen Willis and the rest of the group.

He couldn't face her. Not yet.

CHAPTER TWENTY-EIGHT

The delivery van turned onto a narrow country road and minutes later the vehicle entered the car park of the wholesalers. The van parked up and Dicko switched the engine off and put the keys into his pocket. He and Yoler looked around the car park and could see seven vehicles parked up.

"We may have guests," Yoler said.

"Dead ones." Dicko grabbed his machete off Yoler's lap. "Those cars have probably been here since the ninth of June last year."

"The ninth of June?"

"The day it started," said Dicko. "Well, the day it was officially announced."

"Not sure what the date was, Dicky Boy."

"It was the last time I saw my wife and daughter. I'll never forget it."

He opened the driver's door and jumped out, with Yoler following suit at the other side. Both approached the main door of the wholesalers, and could see that the once automatic doors were opened.

Dicko stopped by the doors and, using the bottom handle part of the machete, he banged on the doors eight times. The two of them waited a minute, but nothing approached the doors from the inside.

They both looked at one another and entered the establishment.

"Stick together," Dicko said. "Be careful with every corner we approach."

"I have done this kind of thing before," Yoler whispered. "On my own."

They could see that the place had been raided many times. A lot of the shelves and areas in the floor were empty, but now useless household appliances like washing machines, hoovers, and dishwashers were still sitting where they had been placed a year ago and left untouched.

The aisles were low and they could see that the floor looked Canavar free. Dicko pointed at the far corner of the large place, where there was some produce. The two of them walked over to the area and could see that the produce was tins of food and bottles of sparkling and tonic water all wrapped up. The products were on pallets, and to their right was half a pallet of breakfast cereal bars.

"Too good to be true," Dicko said.

"I know." Yoler nodded in agreement. "This place doesn't have a single body or a smear of blood."

"And yet the doors are open."

"I know."

"Weird." Yoler scratched at her Beatle haircut and looked baffled. "Maybe someone cleaned up. Maybe it was a base for a group, but they had to leave."

"And leave that?" Dicko pointed at the two pallets.

Yoler hunched her shoulders and took a slow walk away from the pallets and Dicko, and took a look down the tall aisles.

"Right," Dicko called over to Yoler. "We better make a start and move this stuff. It may take a while, even using the trolleys."

"I have a better idea." Yoler beckoned Dicko over to her side. He did as he was told and stood next to his female companion and they looked down the gap, in-between the two tall aisles. A Komatsu battery powered forklift truck sat in the middle of the aisle, and Yoler was the first to react and went over to it. She put her blade on her lap once she was sitting on the truck and could see two levers to her left. One to raise and lower the forks, and the final lever controlled the tilt of the forks.

"It probably doesn't work," Dicko said.

Yoler pressed her foot on the pedal and it moved forwards a few yards until she released her foot. She began to giggle.

"This is unbelievable," said Dicko. "Can you drive it? I can have a go, if you want."

"How difficult can it be?"

The truck moved and Dicko took a step to the side as Yoler drove over to the pallets and stopped. It took her a while to work it out, but she lowered the forks and moved forwards slowly, the forks going under the pallet. She raised the forks, lifting the pallet, then tilted them towards her.

"Go and open up the van, Dicky Boy," she said. "I'm just gonna load these two bad boys straight into it."

Minutes had passed and the back of the van was filled. The two of them had one walk around the place and then decided to leave. Unlike runs from the past, this had been unusually unproblematic and the two of them had even been given a massive slice of luck.

"We'll park this van at a picnic area. It'll be a few hundred yards walk to the camp, but to empty it, everyone is gonna have to muck in and help transport the food."

"How are we going to hide a van when we've parked it up?"

"We can't." Dicko slowed the vehicle down and turned left at a junction. "Thankfully, the picnic area is surrounded by trees, so you won't see the van by just driving along the road. You have to actually go into the area."

"Dicko." Yoler pointed up ahead and could see four of the dead in the middle of the road, with their backs to them.

The dead turned around once their ears picked up the sound of the engine, and Dicko floored the accelerator. The van struck all four and the bodies went under the wheels of the heavy vehicle, decapitating one of them.

Yoler looked to the driver and said, sounding unimpressed, "You enjoyed that, didn't you?"

"A little." Dicko smiled.

"A stupid thing to do."

"I know. I'm sorry."

Dicko still had a smile on his face and was unashamed about his behaviour. He was an experienced survivor with a van full of food that could keep the group alive for another month, and instead of slowing down and driving around the dead, he chose to run the risk of running them down.

Just under ten minutes later and they parked up the van in the picnic area. It was time to move the produce.

*

Helen returned to the camp and Gavin was the first person to realise something was wrong. Helen Willis looked flustered, there was no bucket, and Donald Brownstone was nowhere to be seen.

Gavin was sitting with Grace and they both approached Helen.

"Where's David?" were the first words to come out of Helen's mouth. She looked around the spacious area and couldn't see her son or Lisa anywhere.

"It's okay." Gavin tried to appease the stressed woman. She looked shaken and jittery. "He's in the cabin with Lisa."

"Oh." As soon as Gavin had informed the woman of her son's whereabouts, she began to relax a little.

"Helen," Grace spoke up and placed her arm around the shaken woman. "What's wrong? Where's Donald?"

Helen shuddered, lowered her head, and began to sob. Grace and Gavin looked at one another, scared at the answer she was going to give them. Had he been attacked by a Canavar? Did he have an accident? Where was he?

"I don't know where he is," she finally answered Grace's question. "I don't care either."

Grace and Gavin took a concerned look at one another and Gavin asked Helen what had happened.

"It was stupid." Helen shook her head in disbelief. "It escalated out of nothing."

"What went on?" Grace asked.

Helen wiped tears from her eyes with her fingers and puffed out a breath. She looked over to the cabin, seeing that the door was closed, and pointed over to the area where they usually ate.

"Sit down," she said. "I'll tell you."

CHAPTER TWENTY-NINE

Donald Brownstone was out of breath after reaching the top of the hill and looked at the place that used to be his home for a few weeks.

He looked at the short-lived vegetable patch that Yoler had tirelessly worked on, and he managed a shake of the head.

"This place could have been so special," he muttered under his breath. Despite being voted to leave by the residents before it burned down, he would have preferred Helen and David to live in a normal place, rather than some smelly cabin in the woods.

Donald released a depressed breath out when he turned, and his eyes clocked the two graves of father and daughter. He was never a big fan of Simon Washington, but Donald didn't want this for the man. To lose his daughter and then lose his own life weeks later was a punishment that Donald wouldn't have wished for his worst enemy.

Brownstone gazed at the two shallow graves and was pleased that they were still intact. Even the small cuddly toy that sat on Imelda's grave was still there. Lambie.

Donald's thoughts went back to his altercation with Helen. He was appalled by his behaviour. He had lost control. He loved the woman, but he feared that she would never trust him again. Simon was dead, and yet Donald still couldn't compete with him.

He walked by the burnt-out farmhouse and passed the Mazda. Carrying his knife, Donald went to the front of the house and stopped when he reached the country road. He didn't want to leave his camp indefinitely, but he needed to walk somewhere without getting lost. He decided to turn left and walked along the country road. Despite the reason why he was on his own, it felt good to be out in the fresh air. The wind was more vociferous than it had been in weeks, and the cool air that glided over his frame felt glorious to his overheated body.

His boots felt heavy as the road ascended and once he reached flat ground, Donald decided to take a rest. He walked over to the side of the road and sat on the grass with nothing but fields behind him.

He lowered his head and stared at the tarmac, still thinking about his behaviour, and if Helen would ever speak to him again. He was exhausted. He put his blade into his pocket, brought his knees up, put his arms on his thighs, and rested his head on them. It wasn't planned, but stupidly Donald Brownstone fell asleep. It was only for a few minutes, a power nap, but he did something that any experienced survivor shouldn't have done. He soon woke up when the sound of dragging feet could be heard to his left. Donald looked and saw one lone Canavar stumbling along the road, heading Donald's way.

Donald patted his pockets and felt the knife. He took the blade out and stood up, waiting for the Canavar to approach him.

The dead was a female. It had on a torn dirty dress. Donald could see the polka dot pattern, but was unsure what its original colour was when the woman had put on the clothing many months ago. The dress was torn at the bottom and the neck area was also torn, exposing a rotten breast.

Donald winced, looking at the being, and paused once it was only a matter of yards away. He put his knife back into his pocket and grabbed her arms as she was now inches away, and gazed into the dead face. Her eyes were almost black and she gnashed at the forty-three-year-old man, desperate to take a bite out of his face or neck. Donald wondered why he was trying to survive. What was the point? To go day to day, scavenging for a meal? He saw Helen and David as his family, and had managed to mess that up, so why continue? So he could be with people he had no feelings for? He hardly knew Grace and her mother, Lisa. Gavin was a young man that he was civil to, but they had never been friends.

He had blown it with Helen, and as for Yoler and Dicko ... they were just people he put up with. All he had to do was let go of this dead female and it'd be all over for him. But would he really want to go through that pain? He was always frightened of being attacked and turning in the past, so why was he thinking this way?

"You don't want to die, Donald," he scolded himself. "You're just upset."

His ears twitched and he could hear a noise over the sound of the dead woman growling. It sounded like engines. He threw the woman to the ground and pulled out his knife. The sound of the engines was growing and getting closer. The dead woman tried to get to her feet, but Donald ran and kicked her in the head, then brought his heel down, crushing her face. He dragged the body to the side of the road and looked around. Fields surrounded the man, so he opted to climb the small fence to his left and lie down in the long grass, waiting for the potential danger to pass.

He lay down in the grass, paranoid about what surprises could be around him, and was still clutching his knife. He lifted his head slightly to get a look as the engines approached, and although it was a risky thing for him to do, his intrigue was strong.

Five bikers went by him and he gazed in awe as they followed the bend and disappeared from view. Donald was hopeless with bikes, but they looked like Harleys.

The five men that were on the iron beasts were dressed the same, denim cladded, and were riding bikes with high handle bars. Donald wasn't sure if they were good people or not, but they definitely looked like part of a gang. Whether it was just the five of them, or they were a part of something bigger, he had no idea, but it was something he hadn't seen before. He had come across stray people before, he had run ins with people that claimed to be a part of a community with someone called Orson, and he had heard of the meat wagons, but this was new for Donald Brownstone.

"That's something different." He stood to his feet and brushed himself down. "Where to now, Donald?"

He looked around and began to walk to the country road. He had no idea where he was going.

CHAPTER THIRTY

Lisa Newton rested her back against the wall of the cabin, sitting on the bed, and asked David if he wanted a break. It was dusky in the cabin, and the pair of them could hardly see a thing, but earlier David wanted to go inside, away from the sun.

"Okay," Lisa said. "Shall we do more sums or spelling words?"

"Um..." David paused and said, "Lisa?"

"Yes, buddy."

"Is there any point doing this?"

"I believe so," Lisa said.

"Why?"

"Because I believe that the world will eventually get back to normal. Anyway, it's still good to get some kind of education, but it might be a bit different to what you used to get at school."

David looked puzzled and asked Lisa what she meant by that comment.

"Well..." Lisa thought for a moment. "Eventually you'll be shown life skills."

"What's that?" David still had confusion scrawled over his face.

"Well, I suppose in the old days it was going to the shops by yourself, doing jobs around the house ... that kind of thing. Now it's learning how to filter water, making fires, setting up snares, gutting animals that you've caught, and..."

Lisa could see that David didn't understand half the stuff she was talking about and decided not to continue.

"Donald will probably teach you that kind of stuff," she said.

"Do I need to learn all that?"

Lisa placed her hand comfortingly on David's shoulder and said, "Yes, because one day you might be on your own."

David narrowed his eyes and looked at Lisa. "Why would I be on my own?"

Lisa Newton decided not to continue with her talk. David wasn't her son and it wasn't her place to inject some realism into the way that David thought. Obviously the little man knew he was living in a dire situation, but it appeared that his mother and some others had been protecting him from the horrors of this new world. Maybe that was the right thing to do. Maybe Lisa shouldn't say anything and just stick with spelling and times tables.

"Right." Lisa clapped her hands together. "I think it's time for a break, don't you?"

The young man nodded and said, "I need a drink of water."

"Me too."

Lisa got off the bed and held out her hand. David took it and the pair of them headed outside.

*

Gavin and Grace were talking about days of old, when mobile phones were working and when they had friends. The conversation came to a sad conclusion when Gavin talked about Hayley and other camp members.

He had a few things in common with Grace, as far as music was concerned, but the two of them had also recently lost a sister.

Gavin stood up and looked around. "I wonder if Dicko and Yoler are okay."

"I'm sure they'll be fine." Grace also got to her feet and brushed down her bottoms. "They've been out overnight before."

"I wonder where Donald went."

"I dunno," Grace spoke in a whisper, "but Helen has been acting weird since she came back."

Gavin could see Lisa and little David leaving the cabin and looked over at Lisa who was preparing the soup.

"I was gonna go for a walk," Gavin said to Grace. "Fancy it?"

Grace bit her bottom lip and looked over to the three by the fire.

Gavin laughed, "They'll be fine. I just want to get away for ten minutes. Be in different surroundings."

"Okay then," she sighed.

Gavin walked over to the three sitting individuals and told them that he and Grace were going for a walk. Lisa gave her daughter a suspicious look and Grace explained to her mum that they were both bored.

"Don't be long," Lisa warned.

"Don't worry," Grace said. "We're both carrying knives."

"Don't worry? I've already lost one daughter, I don't want to lose another."

"I'll look after her, Mrs Newton," Gavin said with a smile.

The two walked into the plantation and looked behind. Gavin smiled as he clocked Lisa staring at him, but her face soon disappeared as the pair of them walked further into the woods.

"Your mum was acting weird," he told Grace.

"She's just worried." Grace tucked her greasy brown hair behind her ears. "I'm all she's got left."

Gavin nodded. He understood. He didn't know what it was like to be a parent, but could understand why Lisa Newton was so concerned.

"That ditch is further up," Gavin spoke up.

"Shall we go and see if there's anything in there?"

"If you like." Gavin then pointed at a tree and told Grace that there was a snare near that area.

Grace held back and decided to walk alongside Gavin Bertrand, and they were soon near the ditch that Gavin had fallen in earlier. Gavin told Grace to be careful as they went by it and he felt Grace's hand on his waist as they passed it.

"Where are we actually going?" Grace asked.

"Just for a wander," he replied. "It's good to get out, don't you think?"

"Let's not go out the woods though, Gavin. I don't want to be on the main road."

"You're joking?" Gavin turned and put his arm around Grace. "That's exactly where we're going. You get a great breeze on the country roads."

"You get a great breeze at the pond."

"But we go to the pond every day," Gavin groaned. "A few more minutes and we'll be there."

Their feet trudged through the bracken and Grace could see that the trees were beginning to thin out. The road was near.

They stepped out into the open air and Gavin opened his arms, airing his clammy body.

"You're all sweaty under your arms." Grace giggled and pointed at the sweat patches. "Another trip to the pond for a wash for you, I think."

Gavin playfully grabbed Grace's arm and called her a cheeky cow. She slapped him on his shoulder and their eyes met. Their giggling had ceased, their smiles were gone, and both leaned in and kissed. Before things could go further, if it was ever going to, a noise coming from the woods at the opposite side of the road could be heard. The two broke away and gazed in the direction of where the noise was coming from.

Gavin pulled out his knife, but Grace urged the man to go back into the woods and to the camp. He wasn't listening.

"Gavin." Grace tugged on his shirt. "Come on. Let's go."

Gavin lowered the knife and decided that Grace was right. The safer option was to go back, rather than stand and face what was about to exit the trees.

The two turned and headed back to the camp, but a voice, a familiar voice, had stopped them in their tracks.

"Wait up!" the voice yelled.

Grace and Gavin gasped and looked at one another.

"It's Donald," Grace spoke aloud.

Donald Brownstone could be seen in the distance, twenty feet away, and they waited for him to reach the road.

"Alright guys?" Donald stepped onto the tarmac and raised his hand.

"Where have you been?" Gavin asked the man.

"Never mind that," Donald said. "Let's get to the camp. I'm bloody parched. My mouth is drier than a nun's gash, you dig what I'm sayin'?"

CHAPTER THIRTY-ONE

"Shouldn't be long now," said Dicko.

He slowed the vehicle down and came to a crossroad. He went straight across and looked to his side. His passenger hadn't spoken for minutes and the driver asked if she was okay.

She nodded and revealed a smile, but it was a sad smile.

"What's wrong, Yoler?"

"Nothing, Dicky Boy," she groaned. "I was just thinking."

"Careful," Dicko chuckled. He looked at his passenger again and could see she wasn't in the mood for jokes.

The driver dropped the vehicle down to third as they reached a tight bend, and sped up as the road straightened.

"I was thinking about Imelda," Yoler finally spoke. "And Simes, of course."

"It's shit." Dicko nodded. "But losing people is a part of this world now. I suppose it always has been, but even more so now."

"I know that." Yoler huffed, feeling a little patronised. "I stayed with an old woman briefly. I was out on foot and came across a place. The old woman was there. Her husband had been attacked in the first days. It was just her and her dead husband. He was wandering about in the back garden while she was in the house."

"That's not a story I'm familiar with," Dicko said, checking his side mirror. "When was this?"

"A few months in." Yoler shrugged her shoulders. She wasn't entirely sure. "I stayed with her for a few weeks. Went out now and again and brought food back to her. Her name was Eileen. She was a lovely old woman."

"What happened?"

"Well..." Yoler released a depressed breath out and added, "I persuaded her to remove her husband. I didn't think it was healthy that he was meandering around the garden, but she told me that before I turned up, she used to speak to him through the glass."

"I suppose that's quite sad."

"It was heartbreaking."

"So ... did she agree to your suggestion?"

"Reluctantly." Yoler nodded. "I took care of him, and the pair of us buried him. It was quite an emotional moment, and Eileen was inconsolable. Even at that age, the two of them loved one another."

"What made you eventually leave?" Dicko turned into the country road, with the woods now to either side of them, and it was apparent that they were going to be parking up very soon.

"A few days after we had buried the man, I realised we needed more food." Yoler paused and cleared her throat. "Anyway, I went out on a run, and when I came back, I couldn't find Eileen anywhere."

"Where was she?"

"I went upstairs and found her in her bed. She had taken an overdose. She had written me a letter, apologising for what she did, but she just couldn't live without her husband."

"That's a shame."

"It was the saddest experience of my life, until what happened to Imelda. And then there was the letter she had written for Simon."

"*Stay strong.*" Dicko nodded. "I remember it."

He slowed the van down and pulled into a picnic area. He brought the vehicle to a stop and pulled up the handbrake.

"So this is the plan," Dicko began. "We fill the bags full of tins, go back to the camp, and get the others to help out."

"What about the van?"

"The van's hidden from the main road. It can only be spotted if someone walks into the picnic area."

"If you say so."

*

Over a period of an hour, everyone, even young David, had helped to transport the food and drink from the back of the van. Donald and Dicko were the last to visit the van. There was still food in there, but the evening was drawing in, making the journey through the woods to the cabin more dangerous, and both had decided to call it a day. The two exhausted men had returned to the van for the last time with an empty rucksack over their shoulder, and filled them. Dicko took a look in the van and could see that there was still a decent amount of supplies left.

"We'll get the rest tomorrow," Dicko said to Donald.

Donald laughed and patted Dicko on the back. "Well done. This is too good to be true, you dig what I'm sayin'? I still can't believe it."

"Not too sure it'll get us through the winter," said Dicko, locking up the van and putting the keys into his pocket. "But it's a great start."

The two men walked into the woods, with their heavy bags over their shoulders, and their tired feet dragging through the bracken.

Donald groaned, "When I get back, I'm gonna sleep for two days."

"That tired, eh?"

Donald nodded.

"What's up with Helen?" Dicko asked out of the blue, taking Donald by surprise. "You two were funny with each other when walking to the camp and back. You hardly spoke, if at all."

"We had a falling out," Donald said with no hesitation. "I was an idiot." He could feel Dicko looking at him, waiting for more information, and Donald didn't feel annoyed. Donald looked at Dicko and smiled. "I'll tell you about it in the morning, after I've apologised to Helen."

Dicko's eyebrows lowered and he stopped walking, holding up his hand.

"What is it?" Donald asked him.

"I thought I heard a noise." Dicko turned around and looked behind him. "I feel like I'm being watched."

"Come on," Donald guffawed. "Let's go back. My stomach thinks my throat's been cut."

"What?" Dicko looked at his companion, hoping he would elaborate on a saying he was unfamiliar with.

Donald moaned, "I'm starving."

CHAPTER THIRTY-TWO

Next Day

The morning passed by nonchalantly and most people spent the hours getting the fire prepared, all salivating at the idea of opening the tins that had been discovered by Dicko and Yoler. All had missed breakfast, apart from young David, and Helen, her son and Gavin had taken a trip to the pond for a quick wash and to collect a bucket of water.

After lunch, some had decided to retreat to the cabin. Donald, Dicko and Yoler still sat around the smouldering fire, Gavin and Grace had gone for a walk in the woods and Helen, David and Lisa were in the cabin.

"I didn't want to mention this in front of David," Dicko began, his eyes looking at Yoler and Donald.

"But...?" Donald was annoyed by Dicko's pause and tried to hurry him along.

"But..." he sighed, "we saw one of those meat wagons on our travels."

Yoler decided to speak up. "The people got out and searched the street we were in. We killed them."

Donald's eyes widened and he took a long slow breath out. "They were definitely cannibals? Not just survivors?"

"Definitely." Dicko produced a solitary and confident nod. "They tried to take someone from the street, and the back of the van was covered in ...well, you can imagine."

"The smell was pretty horrendous," Yoler chipped in.

Donald ran his hands over his face and queried, "And this was during the day?"

"Yes," said Dicko. "So next time you're on the road and you hear as much as a rumble of an engine..."

"I hide anyway," Donald interjected. "Being charitable these days can get you killed."

"The trouble is," Yoler began, "is that we don't know whether that was the only van of theirs. It could be just the one, or there could be a fleet of them and an army of people."

"There'll be gangs of survivors everywhere," Donald sighed. "Look at us. And then there was an incident that I witnessed yesterday when I was out."

"What incident?" asked Dicko.

"I heard engines, so I hid. Seconds later a biker gang went by. A few of them, you dig what I'm sayin'?"

"How can people still find petrol for vehicles after a year?"

"Dunno." Donald laughed and ran the tip of his tongue along the front of his teeth. They desperately needed brushing. "But I'm convinced in a year or so we'll all have to resort to horseback and bicycles."

Dicko leaned to the side and picked up a bottle of water that had been sitting there since last night. He took a swig from the bottle and winced as the liquid went down his throat. It didn't taste the best, but he had had worse.

"Look ... guys," Donald began. "I..."

Donald had paused but Yoler and Dicko waited for what he was going to say. They knew he had something on his mind and waited patiently for him to speak.

Donald gulped, lowered his head and puffed out an anxious breath before saying, "I kind of came onto Helen the other day."

Yoler and Dicko looked at one another.

"You ... *kind of?*" Yoler widened her eyes and elevated her eyebrows, waiting for a response.

"I don't know what came over me, I..."

"Were you aggressive?" Yoler asked. "I noticed that there was a bit of an atmosphere between you and her this morning."

"Maybe I came onto her too strong," Donald admitted and puffed out a depressed sigh and shook his head, still annoyed with himself. "It just got out of hand."

"Thinking with your dick," Yoler jumped in. "Typical man."

"I wasn't thinking with my dick. It's more than that."

"Is it?"

"I think I love her."

"You don't love her, Donnie Boy. You're just desperate to put your ding-a-ling inside her fairy cave."

Donald scowled at Yoler and shook his head. He couldn't be bothered to argue with the woman. Sometimes Donald would think that he and Yoler were quite similar. Both of them could start an argument in an empty room.

The door to the cabin opened and out stepped Helen Willis. She gave a smile to Dicko and Yoler, who returned the silent greeting, and walked towards the woods to their left.

"Where are you escaping to?" Yoler tried to joke.

"I need to get out of that cabin and out of this camp," Helen huffed.

"You want company?"

"No thanks."

Helen walked through the cluster of trees, heading to the pond, and Donald turned and looked at Yoler, gesturing with his head to accompany her.

"You heard the woman," Yoler said. "She doesn't want any company."

"But what she's doing is dangerous."

"Sleeping in the cabin is dangerous, but we still do it."

Dicko stood up before an argument between Yoler and Donald took place, and brushed down his black jeans and checked his leather holster to make sure his six-inch blade with the D knuckle skull crusher was still there. "I'll tell you what," he spoke up. "I'll go and check on her."

"Forget it." Donald now got to his feet. "I'll go. I need to apologise to her anyway."

Yoler shook her head and also stood up. "Not sure that's a good idea, Donnie Boy."

Donald walked away from the defunct campfire and his two camp mates, and walked with brisk strides, heading in the same direction as Helen.

Dicko took a step forwards, but Yoler told him to leave it.

*

Donald Brownstone exited the group of trees and was standing near the pond. Helen was at the other end, standing with her shoulders hunched. The field was behind her and the hill where the burnt out farmhouse sat. He stood still and looked at the farmhouse, revealing a thin but sad smile. He was never his biggest fan, but he thought about Simon Washington and his daughter, and then his mind wandered and he thought about his own son. He took a gulp and headed over to Helen. He had some humble pie to eat.

Helen looked up as he approached, and on her face it was clear that she didn't want to speak to him. He continued to approach her and she turned to walk away.

"Helen!" Donald called out. "Speak to me!"

She began to walk over the field and Donald began to jog over to her. He grabbed her arm and said, "Where the hell are you going?"

Helen turned and slapped the man across his face.

Donald, stunned, took a step back and was finding it hard to process what had just happened.

"Just..." Helen bit her bottom lip and paused before saying, "Just leave me alone."

"I wanted to say I'm sorry."

Helen was fighting back the tears and took in a long breath. She nodded gently and said, "Say what you have to say."

"What happened yesterday..." Donald gulped and struggled for words to finish off his sentence. "That wasn't me. I don't know what happened. We've known each other for a while now. You know I've never behaved like that before."

"You scared me yesterday." Helen wiped her eyes and her face quivered with emotion. "I don't think I can trust you again."

"Look, I'm really sorry. If there's anything I can do..."

Helen Willis put her hands on her hips and said, "Yes, actually, there is."

"What? I'll do anything."

"I'm going to go back to the camp. And I don't want to see your face for a while. And when you do come back, I want you to leave me the fuck alone."

It was a rare thing for Helen to swear and Donald was too shocked to react to Helen's scolding. Instead, he watched in silence as she stormed away from him, entering the trees, and making the short walk back to the camp. Donald tucked his lips in and rubbed the side of his face, still feeling the stinging sensation on his cheek.

He felt like striking out, but instead he made a fist with his right hand and punched the palm of his left. "Idiot."

He exhaled sharply and decided, despite Helen stating that she didn't want to see him anyway, to go for a walk. He needed to walk the stress off. He felt his pocket, to check that a knife was present, and began to walk across the field, through the long grass. He didn't want to go too far. The further he went, the more dangerous it would be for him. Donald decided to go to the farmhouse, have a look around the place, and then make a slow walk back to the camp.

Donald reached the hill and could feel the smarting in his thighs as he made the steep climb, his knees sometimes cracking as he made the slow arduous climb.

Once he got to the top of the hill, he turned his back on the ruined farmhouse and sat his backside down and had to rest. He brought his knees up to his chest and dropped his head, resting it on his knees and trying to get his breath back.

Donald Brownstone quickly moved to tears as his mind cast back to years ago, when life was normal, when his son was still alive. He cleared his throat, wiped his eyes, and got to his feet. He turned to his left and saw the two graves of father and daughter, Simon and Imelda Washington. He went over to the two graves and stared at them with sadness. A minute later, he turned and headed for the back door of the house and wondered whether he should walk in.

He placed his hand on the door handle, but changed his mind and released his hand off the doorknob.

He walked around to the side of the house, where the damaged Mazda sat, and reached the front of the place. He walked out onto the main road and could see it was clear both ways.

He was so annoyed with himself and began to pace the road, going back and forth, muttering expletives. This occurred for minutes and once he looked up, he saw something that he didn't notice before. He stopped moving and could see a van in the distance. It was large, white, and before he could take a step forwards to investigate, he felt a blow to the back of his head.

CHAPTER THIRTY-THREE

Gavin and Grace strolled through the woods, talking about old times. Gavin told Grace that he missed watching football, whereas Grace said that she would give her left arm to spend a day listening to music on her iPhone. He turned and smiled at Grace. She noticed this and asked what was wrong.

"Nothing is wrong." He shook his head. "I just..."

"What?"

"I like you." Gavin could feel himself quiver with fright after saying those three words. "I mean ... I *really* like you."

"Me too." Grace smiled and held out her hand. Gavin took it and their hands clasped together.

"Probably the last thing we should be thinking about or getting ourselves into," said Gavin. "We've both recently lost our sisters, we live in an apocalyptic world and could die any day. Shouldn't really be getting close to anyone really."

"The world may have changed," Grace began, "and people may have changed, but we still have feelings. You said that we live in an apocalyptic world and die any day, but that was still the case years ago. People could die any day back then. I had a friend at school who died in her sleep from heart failure. She was fourteen."

Gavin stopped walking and Grace did the same. They both looked at one another and went in for the kiss. A minute later, they pulled their faces away from one another and both beamed.

"We better go back," Grace said. "Before we do something stupid."

"I could live with that." Gavin leaned in for another kiss on her lips.

"I'm sure you could," Grace giggled. "But I don't think getting pregnant is a great idea in this world we're living in at the moment. I *certainly* don't want to get pregnant, and my mum isn't quite ready to be a grandmother."

"We could do other things." Gavin quickly elevated his eyebrows and his smile grew wider.

Grace opened her mouth to say something, but a noise to their right alerted the pair of them. Both stared at where the noise was coming from, but neither spoke or moved. Gavin took Grace's hand and they slowly made their way, with gentle strides, back to the camp.

"Careful," Gavin warned softly. "Try not to stand on any twigs or make any other kind of noise."

"What do you think it is?" Grace asked in a whisper.

Gavin shook his head. "Dunno. Could be an animal, a Canavar... anything. I'd rather not find out."

"But it might come to the camp, whatever it is."

"I know. Need to tell the others." Gavin cleared his throat, still holding onto Grace's hand and moved through the bracken. "Let's hope that whatever it is ends up falling in that ditch."

Both gasped when more noises could be heard and a fox darted to their side. Grace gasped and then released a laugh.

"Fuck's sake." Gavin smiled and shook his head. "What a pair of idiots."

"Come on," Grace urged Gavin. "Let's go back anyway."

"Okay," Gavin sighed.

*

Yoler sat on the steps of the cabin and watched as Lisa Newton and Dicko were sitting down with young David, telling him watered down stories about their journey over the last year. David had asked the question and both adults were taking their turn on telling him. Not only was David learning about where they came from, but Lisa was learning about Dicko's background and vice versa. Occasionally the two adults would look up and smile at each other, making Yoler a little jealous. Lisa wasn't as good looking as Yoler, but she was still attractive and was of a similar age to Dicko, and both had lost children, so they had a lot in common.

A noise could be heard to the left and Yoler took a peek and saw Helen coming through the trees, but there was no Donald.

Helen walked over to her son and kissed him on the top of his head, then made her way over to the cabin. Yoler shuffled over, giving Helen room to sit next to her, and the two gazed over at David and the two adults, still talking.

"No Donald?" Yoler asked Helen.

"He's gone for a walk." Helen sniffed and lifted her head.

"He said he was going to apologise."

"And he did, but I just can't look at him anymore. He gives me the creeps."

"Look," Yoler released a sigh. "You know me and Donnie Boy have hardly been bosom buddies, but he did really look cut up earlier on."

Helen never said a word.

Yoler continued, "You two not getting on is not good for the camp."

"I know."

"Maybe in time you guys can be friends again, in a couple of weeks or so."

"I doubt it."

CHAPTER THIRTY-FOUR

Donald staggered forwards once he received the blow, but it wasn't enough to knock him out. He was dizzy, his head was smarting, but he was still conscious. He turned around to see a man of average height, no older than thirty, standing with a baseball bat in his hand, now looking very nervous.

Another man from a distance began to jog his way and another individual, this time a female, appeared from the front of the van with a hammer in her right hand.

"So you're the cannibals people have been talking about," Donald snorted. There was no response from either of them. All simply remained silent as they hesitantly made slow steps towards Brownstone. He was almost surrounded.

Donald rubbed his head, winced, and casually put his hand in his pocket and pulled out a steak knife. The three continued to advance, but there was concern on the face on the man with the bat now that Donald had produced a blade.

Without warning, the man from behind him, who also had a knife, ran at Donald. Donald turned and swiped his blade, catching the man in the face. The man fell to the floor, screaming and clutching his face. His left cheek had been slashed open. The baseball bat wielding man brought the bat back and ran at Donald, screaming at the top of his voice. Donald jumped out of the way when the bat came crashing down and swiped at the man's face, but missed by inches. The female stood motionless and Donald could see that she was the driver of the vehicle as she had the keys in her left hand.

The bat swiped again at Donald, missing him by half a foot, and the third strike from the man produced cataclysmic results for himself. Donald stepped forwards and rammed his blade into the throat of his attacker. With the knife still embedded, the man staggered backwards and collapsed to the floor. Donald looked up coldly at the woman and began to advance as her two male colleagues were lying on the road, bleeding over the tarmac. One was injured; the other was dying and had seconds left to live.

She released a caterwaul and swung the hammer at the man, catching him on the shoulder. Donald brought the back of his left hand back and caught the woman in the face. She hit him again, this time in his side, taking the wind out of his lungs. Donald staggered back as his female assailant continued to lash out and took another blow to the side of his face. The world span and Donald's legs went to jelly as he stumbled to the floor. He put his hands in front of him as he fell and his vision was similar to a drunk. He looked up and could see the woman slowly approaching.

She had a hard face, tied back ginger hair, and her teeth had been neglected, like most folk. Donald winced and shut his eyes tight, then opened them again, trying to regain some kind of focus. She stood next to him and he swung his right leg, making the woman shriek, taking her legs away from her. She hit the ground and dropped the hammer, and Donald struggled to get to his feet. He stood up, like a man on a boat in turbulent waters, and could hardly focus because of the blows he had taken.

He swung his boot at the woman as she tried to get to her feet, and caught her in the stomach. She coughed and fell flat on the floor. Donald bent over and picked up the hammer from the ground, almost falling over with the dizziness, and brought it down, hitting the woman in the middle of her spine.

She lay motionless and Donald Brownstone walked his large frame over to the moaning man that was ten yards away, still bleeding over the road because of his facial wound. The man was moving from side to side, but he wasn't moving anywhere. He hadn't gained a yard since he hit the floor. Donald knelt down next to the man and could see the fear in his face. He begged for his life, but Donald shushed him like a baby.

"I'm going to ask you a few questions," Donald began. "If you don't answer them or if I think you're lying... Well, you know what's gonna happen, you dig what I'm sayin'?"

The man nodded, his hand on the wound to his cheek, and said in defeat, "You're gonna kill me anyway. Doesn't matter what I say."

Donald shook his head. "I promise that you'll be spared if you answer a couple of simple questions."

The bleeding man looked at Brownstone and believed what he was saying. "Okay." He nodded. "Ask me anything."

"How many of you are there?" Donald asked with a snarl, clutching the knife with his right hand.

"There used to be eight of us."

"And you ... eat people?"

The man nodded and gulped. "We've only been doing this for a few months. We're starving. We need to eat."

"By grabbing people off the road and taking them back to your place, wherever that may be, and carving them up?"

"It's not something we enjoy. It's a must." The man was unrecognisable as eighty percent of his face was covered in his own blood.

"You said there were eight of you," said Donald, his eyes never leaving the man's face. "What happened?"

"Two of our guys were killed a week or so ago. We tried to snatch this bald guy, but we underestimated him. He killed two of our guys with his own hands. I had to drive away and managed to escape, but this guy ran after the van. He didn't give up so easy."

Donald smiled and guessed that the guy the wounded man was talking about could well be Hando.

"Three others went out with the other van yesterday," the wounded man spoke up. "We haven't seen them since."

"I think I know what happened to them." Donald produced a smile, but his eyes squinted when a sharp pain ran across his head. He was convinced he had concussion. "A couple of friends of mine went out on a run and told me they had killed three people. They had a van and they had snatched a woman that was in the back."

The wounded man's face developed into an angry one. "My wife was in that van."

"No sympathy." Donald stood up straight. "You choose to eat people, then you don't deserve to live."

The wounded man glared at Donald and would have attacked the man if he wasn't so seriously injured.

Donald said, "So you guys are the last. I thought the people in the meat wagons would have been scarier than this. I thought you'd have a fleet of vans, a base in the middle of nowhere, with an army of people."

"The more people, the more mouths to feed."

"True." Donald nodded. He looked over to the woman who had attacked him with the hammer and walked over to her. She was beginning to moan and move. The wounded man watched helplessly as Donald rained two blows to the back of her head, killing her. Donald put the hammer into his belt and went over to the first person he had killed and pulled the steak knife out of his throat. He wiped the blade on the dead man's clothes and walked back over to the wounded man.

"I'm a man of my word," Donald said, and staggered to the side of the road and sat down. "You're free to go."

The wounded man seemed to take an age to get to his feet.

Still holding his face, he peered over to a sitting Donald Brownstone, and then bent over to pick up the keys that the woman had dropped when Donald put her down. He then shuffled his damaged body to the van and took a few minutes before the engine was started.

Donald gazed at the vehicle as it slowly moved away. He then looked at the two dead bodies and then dropped his head in his hands. His head was banging and he decided that it was going to be a while before he was going to move.

CHAPTER THIRTY-FIVE

Hando and young Benny crept through the woods and had spent their time collecting wood for a fire outside. They had scavenged earlier and had managed to find two tins of lentil soup. The tins were out of date but it wasn't going to stop Hando and the youngster from having the soup once it was warm enough. Benny was carrying the wood and Hando searched the ground for mushrooms or berries. He could see that they were approaching the edge of the woods, as the trees were beginning to thin out. Hando was leading the way and could see a person on the road. He held his hand up, stopping Benny from walking. He turned and told Benny to drop the wood and crouch next to him. Benny thought it was an odd request, but did what he was told. Once he crouched next to Hando, he asked what was the matter.

"See that man walking along the road?" Hando pointed.

Benny could see the man. He had his back to them, walking along the road unsteadily, and could see he was a big fellow.

"Is that the same guy we saw the other day?" Benny asked.

Hando nodded.

"Is he dangerous?"

"Kind of." Hando bit his bottom lip and was angered just at the sight of the man. "He and some others killed a friend of mine." Hando decided not to tell Benny the whole truth and that he killed Wazza for disobeying him, and had also killed a man in cold blood, which turned out to be Simon Washington, then burned the farmhouse down as the people inside slept.

The truth was that Hando's pride had been severely damaged. The man that was walking away had the nerve to square up to him, and the people from the farmhouse with supplies had refused to take him and his pals in.

"Where's he going?" Benny asked. "Do you think he's going back to his camp?"

Hando smiled and turned to Benny. "I think that's exactly where he's going. Come on. Let's follow him."

*

Still dazed, Donald walked with weary steps. He had planned on spending the day away from Helen, but then again, he never thought he was going to be attacked. The forty-three-year-old passed the decrepit farmhouse and moved along the country road, the wind occasionally caressing his face. He decided to be on the road for no more than half an hour and then head back to the camp. He rubbed his face and used his fingers to massage his temples. It was a lie down that he needed. His lonely walk had no incidents, although he had turned around on a few occasions, thinking there was someone or something behind him.

His mind wandered during his walk and, for whatever reason, his mind replayed what had occurred many years ago.

Donald and his pregnant partner were fast asleep on a Sunday night and a noise was heard downstairs. Donald turned and could see his partner was dead to the world and decided not to wake her. He crept out of bed, wearing nothing but a pair of shorts, and grabbed his dressing gown that was hanging on the door. He wrapped the gown around him as he walked along the dusky landing, and walked downstairs with hesitancy.

He heard another noise that stopped his progression to the ground floor, and was unsure if the noise was coming from inside or outside. He didn't want to call out. If there was somebody in his house, he wanted to catch the bastard.

He moved again and reached the ground floor, and came face to face with the intruder. The red mist had come down on Donald Brownstone. He worked for a living and this piece of shit had broken into his house to take what Donald had worked for.

A scuffle occurred between the men and the lone burglar pulled out a knife. Donald managed to prise the knife out of the man's hand and the burglar escaped and ran out onto the street. What he didn't predict was that Donald, now holding the knife, pursued the man down the dark streets. Fortunately for the burglar, he had managed to outrun the angry Brownstone.

Donald shook his head and brought his mind back to an unwanted reality. He turned left, down a road, and knew the area reasonably well. Once at the bottom of the road, he turned left again, and began walking through a field. Another half an hour and he'd be at the pond, not far away from the camp.

His eyes had clocked something to his left. It was something rare these days. He could see a Canavar, lying on the grass from afar. He approached the dead being, careful where he was stepping in case any other surprises popped up, and pulled out his knife from his pocket. Donald stopped walking once he was near, and slowly crouched down to look at the thing. He was only a couple of yards away and could see that this was probably the most rotten Canavar he had seen. It was almost a skeleton, but was decorated with flesh and non-working organs that could be seen.

Donald continued to look as the creature had now spotted him, trying to reach out and grab him. Even now, in the state it was in, it still wanted to devour flesh. Donald rammed his blade into its skull, stopping its movement, and stood up straight.

Donald looked around, still with a heavy feeling that he was being watched, and walked on. Another twenty minutes or so and he'd be back at the camp.

CHAPTER THIRTY-SIX

Yoler and Dicko had decided to do what Gavin and Grace did an hour ago. They went for a walk in the woods. There was no plan for any kind of supply run until tomorrow. The tins had made them comfortable for a few days, although not complacent, and they told Helen, Lisa, Grace and Gavin that they'd be an hour at the most. Gavin gave off a smirk before the two left and, noticing this, Yoler told Gavin bluntly that they weren't sneaking off for sex, making the man blush.

Yoler and Dicko both carried their blades, not taking anything for granted, and both smiled at one another. It was good to be out. The camp provided a good place to sleep and dwell, but monotony came with it, and every now and again people needed to get away from the place during the day.

"That ditch is up here somewhere." Dicko pointed up ahead. "The one that Gavin fell in."

Yoler nodded and said, "We should block it off. Or fill it in."

"You think?"

"Absolutely, Dicky Boy. Remember a few weeks ago when the cabin was surrounded and Donnie sneaked out the side, leading them away and into the darkness?"

"Of course."

"Well, what if he fell down that ditch that night? He would have been fucked. Something like that could happen again."

"I think we should keep it." Dicko cleared his throat and explained his reason. "We should cover the hole up, turn it into a trap, but make some markings to let us know what it is. If a deer falls through the hole … *that* could feed us."

"You might be onto something there, Dicky Boy," Yoler laughed. "You're not as stupid as you look."

Dicko smiled and didn't bite at Yoler's cheeky remark.

They reached the ditch and spent minutes picking up loose branches to put across. Bracken was pulled from the ground, some came out by their roots, and were scattered over the branches. There weren't too many branches, as the design was for something to fall through it, but enough to hide the ditch. From a human perspective it was obvious what it was, as the square covering of bracken stuck out on the ground like a sore thumb, but they were confident it would fool an animal of some kind.

"Probably won't need to make a mark to tell people what it is," Dicko said, wiping the sweat from his forehead with his lower arm. "It's obvious from here what it is."

"Now what?" Yoler looked at her male companion.

"Now we go to the main road, into the open air. I'm sweating like a fat person in a cake shop."

"Lovely," Yoler giggled. "You have such a way with words."

"That's rich, coming from you." Dicko laughed and turned to his companion. "You told me the other day that you'd rather be pumped by a Canavar than Donald."

"You're still upset by that Ewok comment, aren't you?"

"You said a couple of days ago, being with me is like being boned by an Ewok, so yes, I am a little."

"It wasn't meant to be an insult."

"I don't get it." Dicko shook his head. "I haven't shaved in months, my back's hairy and I haven't waxed my chest since the first days, so what do you expect? And as for Ewok... Why a small and hairy thing? Why didn't you say it was like being boned by Chewbacca or a Yeti?"

Yoler began to giggle, seeing Dicko so flustered, and placed her hand on his shoulder. "Don't be so sensitive," she said. "Let's get some air and then go back."

Dicko sighed and trudged towards the main road with a smiling Yoler by his side.

The two had reached the edge of the woods and stepped out onto the road. Dicko smiled immediately once a breeze closed over him, soothing and cooling his face. He stopped moving, lifted his head, and closed his eyes as the wind went by him.

"I hate to spoil your fun," Yoler spoke with a whisper.

"But?" Dicko opened his eyes and turned to look at her.

"Look for yourself." She pointed to her left, down the road.

Dicko's eyes stared and couldn't make out what he was seeing. It looked like a dead animal of some kind, but it was nearly thirty yards away and the two of them wordlessly made their way over. Yoler placed her hand over her mouth as her eyes clocked the half-eaten fawn. Its insides had been pulled away, a gaping bloody hole in its stomach was present, and its black eyes were like doll's eyes.

It was dead, but it hadn't been dead for long.

"What a way to go," Yoler murmured.

"I know." Dicko sighed. "How on earth can these slow fuckers catch a fawn?"

Yoler had no answer for him. It was obviously the work of the Canavars. Humans would have killed the animal and carried it away to be stripped and cooked. Most of the edible parts of the animal, organs and meat, weren't there anymore.

"Just proves that they're still around," Yoler said. "Not far from our own camp."

Dicko nodded. "I think that's always been the case."

"I remember for a few months hardly seeing any. In fact, Simon was so sure their numbers had dwindled that he told Imelda they were all gone."

"They're still around." Dicko looked away from the carcass and looked into the woods, to his right. "I think there's been an influx of these things recently because they go where the food is, like any other animal. Maybe these Canavars are from the city and towns, and there's just nothing left for them anymore. So they're beginning to ... migrate."

Yoler never responded to Dicko's little speech.

Dicko stepped away from the dead fawn and took steps towards the woods that were on the opposite side of the road where they had come from. He could see the backs of seven Canavars, all spread out, shambling away from him. They must have been the ones that had killed the animal, he thought. Seven Canavars!

This was information he needed to tell the others, apart from young David, of course. The security of the camp would have to be improved.

"Come and take a look at this," he said to Yoler.

She stood by his side and could see the seven dead creatures.

"I was thinking about using some of that blue rope we have in the cabin," he said. "We could then put up more tins to alert us, but further away."

"I suppose that would work."

"At least it will give us more time to retreat back to the cabin or away and to the pond."

"I think it'd come in handy for the night times," Yoler began. "But during the day, we can hear one of those clumsy cocksuckers coming from a mile off. And not only that, you can see them through the trees."

Dicko laughed at Yoler's little rant and she asked him what he was laughing at.

"I was laughing at the fact you called them cocksuckers," Dicko tried to explain to his confused companion. "You reminded me of someone I once knew when you said that."

"What about a guard on a night?" she queried, ignoring his remark that she reminded him of someone from the past.

Dicko shook his head. "No point. And too dangerous. The person doing guard duty would be dangerously exposed. What if the person on guard is attacked? It's pitch black—"

"Alright, alright." Yoler held her hands up. "You don't have to go off on one."

Dicko sat down on the grassy bank, at the side of the road, and Yoler did the same.

"Anything wrong?" she asked him.

He shrugged his shoulders and blew out an anxious breath. "Just thinking about the past."

"I know." Yoler smiled and put her arm around the man in his forties. "It comes in waves, doesn't it?"

"Sometimes I forget what they look like."

"Who? Your family?"

He nodded and dropped his head a few inches. "During the day, when we're awake, I forget what they look like. When I dream about Kyle and Bell, I can see their faces. But when Julie is in the dream, I can't. I know it's her, but she's always faceless."

Yoler had no response for her friend and occasional lover, so she remained quiet and allowed him to speak more, if that's what he wanted. He didn't speak for a minute, until he stood up and announced he was going back to the camp.

Fifteen minutes later, they had both returned. Donald was back.

CHAPTER THIRTY-SEVEN

Hando and Benny had arrived at the pond. It was where Donald went before he took a right into the woodland. The two males crept around the pond and Benny couldn't help himself and began to wash his face with the ice-cold water.

"Come on," Hando snarled at the youngster, eager to get into the woods.

"You should try it." Benny smiled and splashed his face once more. "It's amazing."

Hando angrily gestured to Benny to hurry up and the young man jogged over to Hando's side, not wanting to test his patience any further.

"Now where?" Benny asked.

"In there, brother." Hando pointed into the woods. "But as soon as we see as much as a tent, cabin or individual, we stop walking, keep down and stay still."

"And after that?"

Hando hunched his shoulders. "I don't know yet."

The two men were motionless for many minutes. Then Hando began to move without saying a word to Benny. Both men could feel their knives pricking their thighs as they crept through the plantation with hunched backs. Immediately they could see a cabin and people outside of it. Hando shushed Benny and whispered to him that they would have to walk around so they wouldn't be seen. At the moment they were too close, and if they stayed where they were, it'd only be a matter of time before they would be spotted.

Once they had reached a suitable location, both men got to their knees and could see the cabin.

"There's the guy that we followed," Benny spoke with a whisper, pointing at the burly Donald Brownstone. There were three females sitting around a freshly lit fire and a male adding more wood to it. Then Dicko and Yoler appeared out of the cabin, raising a devilish smile from Hando. Yoler was holding the hand of a minor and this sent a rattle down Benny's vertebrae.

"So what's the plan?" Benny asked a question he didn't really want to ask, but he needed to know what was going through Hando's head. Hando didn't answer straightaway and watched as Gavin went into the cabin. He then exited the wooden place with four tins, two in each hand.

"There, brother." Hando pointed at Gavin. "These people have food and, I'm guessing plenty of it."

"If they have so much food, where did they get it from and how did they move it?"

Hando hunched his shoulders, unsure of the answer. He had a few theories, but not a specific answer for his young protégé.

"Maybe they put so many tins in bags and walked back with them," Hando tried to explain to young Benny. "Or maybe they have a vehicle somewhere and they've hidden it."

"Shall we look for it?"

"What's the point?" Hando shook his head. "To sabotage it?"

"You wanted revenge, right?" Benny scratched his head, unsure what was going to happen.

"What's the point of sabotaging it? If they have the keys, we would have the vehicle, the food. Fuck, even the cabin itself once the whole thing dies down."

"I'm not with you, Hando."

"We wait till the evening draws in." Hando put his hand in his back pocket and pulled out a lighter. "Just until it's enough for us to see."

"Shit, Hando. You can't burn the place down. There's a kid there."

"Relax, brother." Hando released a chuckle and could see the consternation on Benny's face. "We've seen the odd Canavar on our travel, haven't we?"

Benny nodded.

"So the plan is..." Hando paused and cleared his throat quietly. "We use the lighter to entice the dead."

"How?"

"We make a fire, hide, and once there's enough, we expose ourselves and they'll follow us. We'll walk to the camp, while they follow us, and bust that cabin door open. They'll pile in and a massacre should take place. If they fight back and a couple are left standing, we take them down. But one thing is for certain, I can't take them all down on my own."

Benny allowed Hando's plan to sink in and began to shiver with nerves. He was cool with killing the dead, even humans if they deserved it, but there was a boy with the group. He couldn't be a part of that. He couldn't be responsible for the death of a minor. He had killed his neighbours in desperation, for his own survival, but this was a minor as well as six other people.

And what for? A few tins from the cabin? The cabin itself? Both?

Hando obviously had some beef with one or two of the residents, but they had done no wrong to Benny.

Benny kept his mouth shut and could see Hando looking up to the sky. The evening was drawing in.

He looked around the ground and picked up a small branch, four feet in length, and asked Benny for his shirt. Without querying Hando, Benny did as he was told. He took his thin jacket off, then his t-shirt, and passed it to Hando before putting his jacket back on and zipping it up.

Hando tightly wrapped the shirt around the branch and then pulled out some bracken and stuffed bits of the bracken into the wrapped cloth.

"We'll wait an hour or so," Hando said. "You get some rest, if you want. We'll wait till it gets darker before we make a move."

"And then what?"

"We'll go out of the woods and get this thing lit. The flame will entice the dead and they'll follow us as we walk back into the woods and into the camp."

"A bit risky." Benny's words were soaked in doubt and Hando could pick up on the negativity of his younger compatriot.

"Even if we only attract three or four, brother," Hando continued, "it'll be enough to cause a bit of damage to their tiny community. They'll be weakened, and it'll make our job easier if we attack them and their numbers are fewer."

"Attack them? I'm not sure, Hando."

"You remind me of a guy I once knew," Hando said with a chuckle. "His name was Q. He was weak, like yourself, but I can teach you how to survive. I'm surprised you've lasted this long."

"I'm not weak." Benny was finding it hard to control his anger. "I told you about my neighbours, didn't I?"

"That was a bad thing that you did." Hando nodded the once after he finished the sentence. "However, you have to be consistently bad in order to survive long term. There is no karma, and there is no God to judge you. Be bad and you'll survive longer than most. Your conscience is your weakness."

"I can't do it, Hando."

"Brother, listen to me."

Benny was adamant. He snapped. "I *won't* do it." Within seconds, Benny had gone from *can't* to *won't*.

"Okay." Hando released a sigh. "Let's get out of these stifling woods and get some air. I think there may be a road up ahead."

Hando picked up the branch that had Benny's shirt wrapped around it, as well as bracken, and put the branch into the side of his belt.

The two men walked, bags still on their backs, and were out of the woods after a few minutes. Once upon a time the woods in the area were dense and stretched for miles with no interruptions, but that was thwarted when men knocked down a lot of trees to make roads. The woods still stretched for miles, but there were gaps where the roads were present.

Both men stepped out of the woods and onto the road. The carcass of an animal could be seen to their right, but they ignored it and tried to enjoy the cool wind that glided over them.

"It's good to be alive," Hando sighed. "To feel the wind on your face is a blessing, yet people over a year ago took it for granted. You could experience more joys like this, brother, but you need to up your game."

"I've told you." Benny was exasperated and huffed, "For the last time—"

"I know, I know." Hando held up his hand, gesturing to Benny to calm down. "When we first met and you told me you killed your neighbours to survive, I was impressed."

"This is a step too far. Not with a kid there."

"I understand." Hando looked genuinely disappointed. He got closer to Benny and put his arm around the young man and added, "And you definitely won't change your mind?"

Benny shook his head.

"Fine."

Hando pulled out his knife from his right pocket and plunged the blade into Benny's chest, straight through the heart. Benny collapsed onto all fours and Hando flipped him over. Benny was now lying on his back. Hando reached and pulled out the blade, and then wiped the steel on Benny's clothes.

"Sorry, brother." Hando placed the knife back into his pocket, took the branch out of his belt, and took a seat on the grassy bank as Benny's corpse lay in the middle of the road. "I really am."

CHAPTER THIRTY EIGHT

Donald sat on the side of the bed where young David lay and smiled at the young man. The cabin was dark and he could just about see the boy. Helen had been in and tried to settle the boy, but he asked for Donald, a man that David had grown attached to over the months.

Donald went in after Helen made the announcement. It was the first time she had spoken to the man, but she did it only because she had to. Once Helen sat down with the rest of the group, all talking about stories from the past, Donald was inside and it was just him and David.

"How are you feeling, little man?" Donald asked the boy.

"Not bad." David took in a deep breath and released a heavy sigh for such a young boy. "I was just thinking..."

"What about?"

"About everything."

Donald could hear the emotion in the child's voice, but decided to keep quiet and allow David to speak further when he was ready.

"I was thinking about dad." The young fellow paused for a moment and then added, "I sometimes forget about him. I don't think about him everyday. Do you think about your son, Donald?"

The question took Donald by surprise and the burly man could feel his throat tighten. Donald gulped hard and replied, "Yeah. I think about my son every day, every hour of every day."

David lowered his head and wiped his eyes. "When mum was in here, I became a little upset."

"Did you, little man? Why?"

"I know you two aren't getting on. I can sense it."

"Oh." Donald lowered his head and patted David's legs. "To be fair to your mum, I'm not the easiest person to get on with."

"I know, Donald. I sometimes hear some of them out there talking about you, when you're not here, saying bad things about you."

Donald released a gentle laugh. "Is that right?"

"I was thinking about Imelda earlier and then the people that used to live here. Especially Hayley, Jamie and Gary."

"Well, hopefully something like that won't happen again. The trouble is, there's danger wherever you stay."

"What do you mean?" David began to sit up and leaned his back against the wall. "Are you talking about the Canavars and dangerous people?"

"I'm talking about locations." Donald cleared his throat and wiped his nose with his thumb and forefinger. "You see, it doesn't matter where you stay, there's always going to be hazards. If you stay in the country, there's less people and the dead, but also less places to go to for supplies. Kind of frustrating if you don't have the wheels. Thankfully, Yoler and Dicko brought back that van. If you live in the city, the amenities are better, but densely populated places means more of the dead and more desperate people. Being in the woods keeps us hidden, but it still has its dangers."

"Like when the Canavars came and we had to flee?"

"Exactly."

A silence enveloped the two and Donald stroked the boy's head.

"I hope you're feeling better," the boy moaned.

"Feeling better?" Donald stopped stroking the boy and narrowed his eyes in confusion.

"Yeah. That's how you got those bruises, right?"

Donald was unsure how David knew about his tussle with the three individuals, let alone the meat wagons, and opened his mouth to query the boy, but David began to explain before Donald could get the words out.

"I overheard Dicko and Yoler talking."

"What did you overhear?"

"I heard about the meat wagons, people who kill others for food."

"You overheard or you eavesdropped?"

David never answered, telling Donald that it was probably the latter.

"There were people out there that did those things," Donald began to explain to the minor. "But they're not around anymore."

"I know. You killed some and Yoler and Dicko killed some before."

"Oh. You know about that as well, eh?"

"Is that really how you got your bruises? You told me you'd fallen over."

"Yeah, well..." Donald didn't know how to respond to the boy and stayed silent for a bit before saying, "Get to sleep. I'm gonna join the rest outside."

Donald stood up and bent over to kiss the boy on his head. Once he did this, they both exchanged 'goodnights' and Donald walked away, heading for the door.

"Donald?" the boy called out.

"Yes..." Donald nearly called David by his own son's name and had to bite his lip.

"I don't care what they say about you. I'll always like you."

"Thanks," Donald snickered.

He shut the door behind him and sat on the steps of the cabin once he was outside. He looked over to the group around the fire and clocked Dicko's face. Dicko used his head to beckon Donald over, but Donald smiled and shook his head. He was happy where he was.

He wanted to get Helen on her own. He wanted to apologise to her, but the last thing she wanted was to be alone with Donald Brownstone. She had her back to him and turned around. He smiled thinly at her, but her face remained hard and without emotion. She turned back around to converse with the rest of them and Donald continued to sit alone.

"Fuck it," he muttered under his breath.

He stood up and went back into the cabin. He was going to talk to young David for a while longer and then turn in for an early night. There was nothing else to do.

An hour later, everybody had turned in.

*

Hando had been whistling a tune on and off for the last twenty minutes, and could at last hear movement coming from the woods opposite where he was sitting. He stopped whistling and stood up. Taking his branch with him, he retreated to the woods behind him, crouched down behind a tree, and looked over the road to the woods on the other side. A Canavar staggered out from the trees and stumbled out onto the road. But it wasn't alone; two others were following behind.

Hando smiled on seeing this and decided to leave them be for now, hoping one or two more would appear for the feast. The first Canavar spotted the body of Benny lying on the floor, and dropped to its knees once he was by the corpse and began to feast. The other two had now exited the woods and made their way over to Benny.

"Three." Hando grinned and released a light chuckle. "That should do. That should cause a bit of damage, and then I'll kill the rest myself." He patted his pocket where his knife was. "That's if there are any left."

Now all three were on their knees, pulling out Benny's insides and stuffing the bloody findings in their mouths. Two more emerged from the woods and copied the three before them. The first three that emerged from the woods were male, but these two were female. One had a torn and ripped yellow summer dress, but the other had lost her clothing and wore nothing but a dirty bra and pants.

Hando twisted his face when he clocked the discoloured body of the woman and got a waft from the rotten walking corpses. He would never get used to that smell.

He waited and waited, and could see that the sky was dimming, and if there were clouds in the atmosphere, it would have been darker. He had no idea of the time, but guessed it was probably around eight or nine

As the first Canavar stood up straight, looking like it was ready to leave, he pulled out his lighter and lit the branch that had the bracken and

Benny's t-shirt tightly wrapped around it. It took a while before the head of the branch was on fire, and once Hando was confident the gentle wind that was present wouldn't blow out the flame, he stood up and began to wave the branch gently from side to side. One by one the flame was noticed, and almost a minute later all five Canavars were walking away from Benny's body and heading towards the flame, towards Hando.

"Come on, you smelly bastards. Follow your Uncle Hando."

He waved the branch and began to make small backward steps into the woods. Once the five ghouls were in, he turned and jogged his way through the trees and turned to see how close they were. They were ten yards behind him but were all trying to follow him. The five were making a sufficient amount of noise and he hoped that this wouldn't be heard by the people in the cabin. The security system had been removed by Hando earlier, by simply cutting the rope and allowing the tins to fall to the floor. It wasn't difficult.

He ran ahead and was near the spacious part of the woods where the cabin was based. It looked like everyone had turned in. The five Canavars weren't far behind. Hando crept to the cabin and went up the steps. As soon as the five began to stagger their way to the cabin, Hando tried the door, but it was locked. He kicked the door in and grabbed the first Canavar and threw it inside and then did the same with the second.

He climbed to the roof of the place, two Canavars were inside the cabin and three were making their way up. Screams filled the place and a grinning Hando threw the branch away, jumped off the roof of the cabin, and began to make his way back into the woods. He hid in the darkness, behind one of the trees and watched the carnage unfold.

CHAPTER THIRTY-NINE

Dicko's dreams were plagued by horrors of the past year. In his dream he was staying at Sandy Lane, a place where he had stayed for a month with people he had met after the apocalypse had broken out.

The dream wasn't fictional; it was a replay on an event that really happened some eight or nine months ago. At this point he had lost his daughter and wife, but still had his son. Dicko had a shotgun as the two of them had gone for a walk along the field in the large secure camp, and his son Kyle was bursting for the toilet. Dicko told him to go where they stood whilst no one was looking, but the little boy didn't want to.

Kyle ran over to the changing rooms, at the other side of the field, and Dicko went looking for him once he realised his son had been away too long. He bumped into a fellow resident called Karen, told her the predicament, and the pair of them entered the changing rooms. He knew the changing room door was stiff, so Kyle may have unwittingly locked himself in and couldn't get out.

His mind produced vivid images of him pushing the door of the changing room open as wide as it could get, spilling daylight into parts of the room. Karen, the woman that was with him, quickly turned away from the door and felt sick from the smell that hit them both. The foul stench tortured Paul Dickson's nose, but his concern for his seven-year-old son was more of a worry for him. *Poor thing's probably frightened to death being alone in the dark, unable to find the door to get out.* His face then twitched as he took in a deeper breath. *Jesus, it stinks in here.*

He called out his son's name, but received no answer. Paul and Karen both stepped inside. Paul, holding the shotgun loosely in his right hand, constantly called out Kyle's name, but there was no response. He wasn't by the urinals, and Karen began checking under the cubicles, but nothing was there. Paul and Karen both had their t-shirts over their noses as they walked into the shower area, and Karen peered her head round to look in. She suddenly released a scream.

Paul barged past Karen, and felt his knees buckle once his eyes clocked the macabre and surreal sight of one of the dead, sitting down on the shower floor and stuffing entrails from a body into its mouth. His knees began to buckle and his face drained. The thing was aware that other entities were in the room, but the 'meal' he was enjoying appeared to be too good to be dragged away from.

It hadn't sunk in just yet for Paul Dickson, but as soon as the sitting beast put its hands inside the torso of the little body once more, he dropped the shotgun and his whole body shuddered. Karen held him back and gently pushed him out of the shower area. He fought back, and re-entered the area to help his boy, despite him being *beyond* help, and clocked the awful sight of little Kyle's body and his bloody face, his hazel eyes wide open.

Karen picked up the shotgun off the floor, went over, and front-kicked the creature off the body. She walked around and grabbed the snarling beast by its hand and pulled it across the floor with her left, whilst holding the shotgun with her right. It grabbed her ankle as it writhed on the floor, still chewing parts of Kyle, and she gave it a smack in the face with the butt of the gun, turned it around, and emptied a shell into its face.

Its face exploded; the contents were spread over the floor. The noise was deafening; both Paul and Karen's ears were ringing, and she dropped the gun to the floor next to the mushy brains that had been forced out of the creature's head. She took a quick peep at the remains of young Kyle Dickson, his belly had almost been emptied, and sobbed as she went back over to the shell-shocked father who was still standing at the end of the shower area, unsure what to do.

Paul walked backwards until his back was against the tiled wall of the changing room. Tears streamed down at a furious rate and his face wobbled. He slowly slid down, sobbing uncontrollably because he had lost his son. His strawberry blonde hair would never be sniffed again by his father. Paul would never get the chance to look into Kyle's hazel eyes, or wake up next to him anymore. And Paul's elbow would never be pinched and twisted again by his little man, the way Kyle used to whenever he was nervous.

After that, Dicko had lost his mind for a while. Sandy Lane was then attacked by the dead, and the surviving residents left to go to a place in Little Haywood, to a street called Colwyn Place, where another community had been set up.

*

A scream filled his ears, but this time it wasn't something from his dream. His eyes suddenly widened and he remained lying on the floor, almost paralysed.

Another scream pierced the night, coming from a female, and Dicko quickly got to his feet and stood up in the darkness. More screams and scared voices filled the cabin, and the sound of Donald's tone was heard, telling everyone to back up into a corner.

A pair of hands grabbed Dicko by the throat and from the coldness of the hands, the snarling, and the stench, he knew straightaway it was a Canavar.

"Canavar!" he cried.

He grabbed it by its shoulders and pushed it back. A small light appeared from the corner of the cabin that lit up the place. Dicko turned around to see Donald holding a match and he lit a candle. Three of the dead were inside, a body was on the floor, and Dicko reached for his knife whilst Yoler appeared from nowhere and lashed out at the first one with her own large blade. Her blade embedded into its skull as voices and cries of panic filled the cabin, and Dicko used his foot to push the other two out of the cabin, both Canavars falling over and tumbling down the steps.

Dicko stood in the doorway and waited for them to climb back up. Yoler emerged by his side, and with what little light they had, they could see four of them.

"Fuck this!" Yoler cussed and trotted down the steps with her stained blade at the ready.

She swung at the nearest one and Dicko had now reached ground level and put down one of the dead. Two left and simultaneously they pulled their blades behind their heads and brought them down at the top of the skulls of the remaining two. Yoler's 'victim' stood motionless and eventually slumped to the ground in a heap, whereas Dicko front kicked the Canavar he had just destroyed, pushing it backwards and freeing the blade.

They turned around and could see Donald dragging out the Canavar from inside the cabin and angrily throwing it onto the ground. Cries continued from inside the cabin and Dicko told Donald that the rest inside had to be quiet in case any more turned up. They had killed five, but they were surrounded by darkness and unaware if any other dangers were lurking about.

"Keep them quiet?" Donald huffed. "Easier said than done. If we knew what was happening, we could have used the side door to escape, like I did a few weeks ago, remember?"

Dicko sighed, "I know they're scared—"

"Scared?" Donald almost released a laugh. "You haven't seen what's happened, have you? Helen wouldn't even let me go near David. They're all in shock in there."

Dicko and Yoler both looked perplexed and never responded verbally.

"Go and take a look inside. I'll stay here."

Dicko and Yoler put their blades away, into their belts, and went inside the cabin, whilst Donald remained outside with his knife out and in his right hand.

Yoler and Dicko stopped once they were in the middle of the cabin and could see Helen and David cuddling one another in one corner, crying. In the other corner of the place they could see a hysterical Grace consoling her mother. Lisa Newton had been bitten on the neck. Blood poured out of the woman and she had minutes left to live if she was lucky. By their feet was Gavin Bertrand. He was dead. He was the first to be attacked and died from neck wounds, similar to what was happening to Lisa.

"Oh, shit." Yoler groaned and rubbed her forehead. She had experience, like Dicko, of witnessing carnage of people she knew and cared about, but it was still heartbreaking to witness.

Dicko remembered his dream and saw a crying David being consoled by Helen. He went over to the corner to see if they were okay, but Helen screamed at Dicko to leave her alone. Dicko was baffled by her outburst and grabbed the candle, and took a step closer to mother and child. He could see the fright on both of their faces and felt for them. Then he saw something that twisted his guts.

He could feel his throat harden and placed the candle back where he had picked it up. He walked over to Yoler's side and whispered in her ear, making the female's eyes widen with shock.

Young David had been bitten on the arm.

CHAPTER FORTY

Donald nervously looked around and could see nothing but darkness. He had an idea who could have been responsible for this, but the people inside the cabin were the primary focus at the moment.

He shook his head and could hear a snap to his left. It was faint, but it was the unmistakeable snap of a twig he had heard.

Another faint noise could be heard and Donald ran into the woods, where the noise had come from and could just about see the silhouette of a man that he was convinced was Hando. Both men were holding a blade and both swiped at one another once they were in close proximity, but both missed. Donald grabbed Hando by the shoulders, dropping his knife and both men fell to the ground. After a minute of wrestling, Hando had managed to overpower Donald and was on top of the man. He rammed his blade into Donald's shoulder, forcing the man to scream out, and took a left hook as he pulled out the blade.

Donald hit Hando again and the dazed man fell back and dropped his knife. Donald scrambled to his feet and could see the silhouette of Hando trying to get up. Donald took a run at the man and kicked him in the stomach and could now hear the voices of Yoler and Dicko calling him from behind. Donald kicked Hando again and yelled, "Over here!"

Donald's ankles were grabbed and he was pulled to the ground. He felt dazed once his head hit the floor and felt the presence of his assailant standing over him.

"Fuck," he muttered. He was convinced he was done for.

The sounds of disturbed plantation could be heard ahead of Donald and it had also been heard by Hando as well. The man pulled out a lighter and the flame lit up a small part of the woods. Two Canavars could be seen making their way in their direction, and Hando grinned.

Donald could hear the voices of Yoler and Dicko still calling out to him, but couldn't respond.

"Why did you do this?" Donald called out. "For the food? For revenge after turning you away at the farmhouse? And then killing your friend?"

"I did it to survive, brother." Hando was struggling to speak between his hard breaths. "If killing you lot … hell … if killing a dozen people is what is needed to help me survive longer, then that's what needs to be done. Children are no exception. It's never stopped me before."

"You raped Grace's mother and killed her younger sister!"

"I didn't say I was perfect, brother, did I?" Hando, still holding the lighter, took a peek behind him and could see the two dead were around ten yards away.

Hando placed his lighter back into his pocket and picked up a large boulder that was sitting in the bracken to the right of him. "Now, brother, I'm going to smash your fucking brains in." He walked towards the lying Donald and lifted the rock above his head. "I won't leave you for the dead. That would be too cruel."

Hando bent over and grinned at the injured Brownstone. Donald didn't cower. He gulped and brought his foot back once Hando was closer and pushed out into Hando's midriff, a second before the boulder was due to be released, and gave every ounce of energy he had left in that one kick. Hando dropped the boulder and staggered backwards a few yards, finding it difficult to stay still, and the silhouette of the man suddenly disappeared from Donald's eyes.

"What the...?"

A light appeared from behind Donald and Yoler and Dicko arrived. Dicko was holding a candle in his left hand with his machete in his right, and all three could see the two Canavars, but Hando was nowhere to be seen.

Yoler pulled Donald up to his feet and told him not to move, as she and Dicko were about to take care of the two dead that were seconds away from the three of them.

Donald looked around the woods and a thought entered his head. "No, wait!" he called out. Donald rubbed his head and went over to the two dead. He pushed them both over, giving them three seconds of respite as the Canavars tried to get back to their feet, and told Dicko to follow him. Donald moved a few yards and now recognised the area. The candlelight revealed a section of the ground, trees ahead of them, but also a large square hole in the ground. It was the trap they had covered, and Donald moved forwards a few more yards to take a look in, and already knew that Hando was gong to be at the bottom of it.

Donald, Dicko and Yoler all peered down and could see a groaning Hando. His left ankle was broken and he had been stabbed in his right thigh by the knife in his pocket after his awkward fall.

The two Canavars approached the three by the edge of the ditch and Yoler and Dicko took a quick peek at Donald. Feeling their look, he told them that the man in the ditch deserved the death he was about to get.

Dicko gave Donald the candle and told him to step to the side as the pair of them put their weapons away and grabbed the two advancing Canavars and threw them into the ditch.

Dicko took a hold of Donald and helped him back to the camp, with Yoler by their side. Behind them were the screams of Hando being ripped apart. It was a death that was beyond cruel, but all three were convinced it was something he deserved, despite not knowing the full extent of the man's horrific wrongdoings over the past year.

CHAPTER FORTY-ONE

A candle was placed on the ground near the cabin, and a dazed Donald fell to his knees. He was told that Lisa and Gavin had perished and that he couldn't go inside because of the mess. Yoler told Donald that she would stay with him, in case there were more Canavars about, and Dicko went into the cabin to assess the situation. A red stumpy candle sat in the corner of the place and the room was filled with crying.

Dicko put his machete away and could see Grace still crying and holding her dead mother in one corner, and in the other, Helen Willis and her son were still.

Dicko walked over to Grace, stepping over Gavin's body, trying not to get blood on the soles of his boots, and crouched down to Grace's level.

"How did this happen?" she cried. "I don't understand."

"It was the same man that killed your sister," Dicko began to explain. "He also had a bit of beef with us in the past as well, especially Donald. He brought Canavars with him and kicked the door open. He wanted to hurt us."

"Why?"

"Revenge?" Dicko hunched his shoulders. He wasn't entirely sure himself. "Maybe he wanted the food that we've got stocked here. Maybe it was for both reasons. He's dead now, thanks to Donald, so don't worry."

"Is Donald okay?"

"He's fine. He's outside."

"How did that Hando know we were here?"

Dicko sighed and was unsure how to answer her query. He wasn't sure, so he guessed and conjured up a few theories. "Maybe he went to the farm and came by us by accident. Maybe he had spotted Yoler and I when we were out and followed us back here, or he had spotted Donald... I'm not sure."

Grace stroked her mum's head and seemed unbothered that she was covered in her blood from her throat wound.

"I'm sorry about your mum," Dicko said. "And Gavin. I know you two..."

"I know."

"The only positive out of this whole mess is that because your mum died from her injuries, from massive blood loss, she won't turn." Dicko stood up and then turned his head to a frightened Helen and gave her a reassuring smile. "I'm going to move Gavin outside. I'll be back in a bit."

Dicko called Yoler in and they both removed Gavin and placed him at the side of the cabin, out of view. They checked on Donald again and could see the man was now sitting up, but still dazed from the blows he had taken during the fight with Hando.

"We need to remove Lisa as well," Dicko said to Yoler. It was a conversation that Donald overheard. "We'll put her next to Gavin."

Donald staggered to his feet and was like a drunken man on a Saturday night. Dicko went over to the man, but Donald pushed him away.

"Leave me alone," he snarled, still looking unsteady on his feet. "I want to see how Helen and David are."

"They're fine, Donnie Boy," Yoler huffed. "Sit down before you fall down."

Donald Brownstone ignored the advice from the female and entered the cabin. He quickly looked at Grace and Lisa's body, but his main focus was Helen and David.

He approached the mother and son, but Helen screamed at Donald to keep away. Her words fell on deaf ears, and Donald crouched down and touched David's head. Helen hugged the sobbing boy tighter and Donald stood up straight and staggered back after what he had just seen.

"Please," Helen begged. "Leave us alone."

Dicko entered the cabin and could see Donald was stumbling. He ushered the man outside and re-entered the place and told Grace that he wanted to move her mother outside. She agreed, and offered to help.

The body was placed next to Gavin at the side of the cabin, and Grace fell to her knees and cried. The two people she was closest to had died in the space of a few minutes. It was a hard one to take for the eighteen-year-old female.

Grace and Dicko walked by the cabin and stood outside and could see Donald sitting on the floor and Yoler on her knees, inspecting something on the ground.

"What is it?" Dicko asked her.

"The rope with the tins has been cut," she said. "That's why we never heard anything approaching."

"He's been bitten," Donald muttered behind them. "The youngster has been bitten."

Dicko cleared his throat and groaned, "Yes, we know."

"How do we handle this?"

"We're gonna have to wait until the boy passes," Yoler began. "Then we need to … take care of him."

Grace continued to sit silently on the floor and stared into space, and Yoler and Dicko's attention turned towards Donald once he did something that the pair of them had never seen before from the big man. He broke down and burst into tears.

Yoler and Dicko helplessly stood and stared at the broken man as he was doubled over with grief. They had no idea he was so close to the boy. But was it just that, or did it bring back the painful memories of when he lost his own son? Yoler took a step forwards, unsure whether to console the man or not. She decided not to. Instead, she watched him crumble and could feel her own emotions beginning to emerge.

A cry of pain from inside the cabin pierced the ears of the four individuals outside, and that cry alone forced Dicko to react first. He entered the cabin, leaving the three outside, and could see a heartbroken Helen Willis.

Dicko crouched down next to the woman, and placed his fingers on David's carotid artery without any objections from Helen.

"He still has a pulse," Dicko said with a hushed tone.

"But I can't get him to wake up. Why?"

Dicko had no answer for the distraught woman and all he could do was shake his head.

"Why?" she persisted. "Why doesn't he wake up?"

There was no point beating around the bush. Dicko had seen this many times before, so he decided to tell her straight. "He's slipped into a coma. He won't wake up now."

"What do you mean?" she cried. "What are you saying?"

"It's only a matter of time," Dicko groaned. "He's going to turn."

Helen shook her head and continually said the word *no* over and over, but she knew that Dicko was right. She knew that the reality was that her baby boy was as good as dead. He was beyond help.

"Listen," Dicko began. "I know you don't wanna hear this right now, but he's gonna have to be taken care of. You know what I mean, don't you?"

She nodded as tears streamed down her face.

"You're gonna have to say your goodbyes pretty soon, because once his heart stops, he'll start to turn."

"How are we going to do this?"

"It's okay. I'll take care of him."

"No, you won't," a voice bellowed from behind, making Helen and Dicko gasp. It was Donald. "I'll do it."

CHAPTER FORTY-TWO

Next Day

It was two minutes after midnight, not that time mattered so much in this new world, and a new day was upon the group of survivors. The candle in the cabin was still alive and flickered, and the one outside that had been placed into the ground was still alive, although it had gone out on a couple of occasions and had to be re-lit.

Helen had spent many minutes clutching her son and kissing his head, refusing to let him go. The longer she stayed with him, the more likely he could turn in her arms. This was something that had to be delicately explained to the woman, and although she understood, she begged for one more minute with her only child.

Donald, the volunteer to put David to rest properly, held his knife in his right clammy hand and crouched next to the distraught mother.

Helen Willis gave her son one last kiss, tears streaming down her cheeks, and reluctantly gave Donald a nod.

She stood up and her legs wobbled, then Yoler entered the cabin and hooked her arm with Helen's and the two females slowly exited the cabin.

Helen collapsed to the floor and broke down. Helen's fall had taken Yoler by surprise and she couldn't hold her up in time as the distraught woman fell.

She was on the ground and being comforted by Grace. The sobbing coming from the mother made Yoler wince for a few reasons. Losing her child must have been the worst feeling in the world. And the selfish reason why Yoler was uncomfortable with Helen's breakdown was that her crying could entice more of the Canavars from afar.

She decided to hold her tongue.

What could she have said? I know you're hurting, but is there any chance you could keep the volume down?

Yoler and Dicko watched helplessly as the two females who had lost a family member consoled one another. Dicko's eyes then turned their attention to the cabin. He couldn't see anything. The door was open, and the candlelight revealed a part of the place, including the foot of the bed, but neither Donald or the deceased David could be seen. Donald was a tough man, and although he loved that boy like he was his own son, he was sure he could put the boy to rest. It wouldn't be easy, but it was the right thing to do.

A minute had passed and Yoler and Dicko hadn't exchanged a single word. Dicko puffed out a breath and headed for the cabin, leaving Yoler standing by herself and the two broken-hearted females on the floor.

Dicko climbed the few steps to the entrance of the cabin and peered inside. Donald was sitting in the corner of the wooden place and had embraced the boy, little David, in his arms. Donald was crying and stroking the boy's head. The scene almost moved Paul Dickson to tears when the memories of his own son's death, nearly a year ago, were brought back to his attention.

Dicko was about to clear his throat to get Donald's attention. He wanted to tell the man to hurry up, as the boy could turn any second, but Dicko quickly spotted the bloody blade by Donald's feet.

The deed had been done.

Dicko left the place, giving Donald some peace, and made slow steps back to Yoler.

"Everything okay?" she asked him.

Dicko nodded. "We need to dig three graves."

*

The three graves were dug at the right side of the cabin. There was only one shovel and the ground was tough, but Donald insisted on digging all three.

Dicko and Donald were the ones to lay the bodies in the shallow grave. Donald looked exhausted, and despite the trauma of the night, he looked like he needed to sleep. They all did.

Dicko offered to cover the bodies with the dug up dirt and Donald agreed and sat down. It seemed cruel that only David was wrapped in a sheet and Gavin and Lisa lay with nothing but the clothes on their back. To pile dirt on their uncovered faces seemed cruel and unjust, and Donald insisted on using his own sheet to wrap David in.

The five remaining survivors stood around the three graves at the right side of the cabin, three of them in tears. Yoler and Dicko, the only ones that weren't in tears, looked at one another. They were both thinking the same thing. It sounded heartless. But the longer they stayed outside, with the sobbing and the light from the candle, the higher the likelihood of more Canavars turning up.

Eventually, people decided to turn in, and both grieving females shared the bed, sobbed gently, and hugged one another. The candle from outside was blown out and all five went into the cabin and Dicko placed a small cabinet against the door because the lock had been broken when Hando had kicked it in.

This whole scenario brought it back to Dicko when he had to bury his own son. He remembered being at Sandy Lane, with his friends to either side of him. Kyle Dickson had been tightly wrapped up in sheets, and had already been placed into the shallow grave that was just over three feet in depth when Dicko had arrived.

He remembered most of the people's names that were there. There was Lee James, Rick Morgan, Bentley Drummle, a girl called Sheryl, Charles Washington, Henry Winter, Garth Bateman and Jon Talbot. Dicko remembered a woman called Rosemary who stood behind with a young sobbing girl called Lisa, and a woman called Gillian Hardcastle was standing next to a tearful young woman called Jasmine Kelly.

After the few words were spoken, a young girl called Lisa sang the opening lines to Stevie Wonder's *You are the Sunshine of My Life,* a song that Dicko and his wife used to sing to Kyle, especially when he was a baby.

Yoler and Dicko sat at the side of the cabin with the other three at the other end. Donald was lying on the floor with his hands behind his head, staring up at the ceiling. Helen and Grace held each other on the bed. The red stumpy candle was slowly diminishing the longer it burned, and Dicko asked the four of them if he could blow the candle out as they all needed to rest, despite the extremely difficult circumstances Grace and Helen were experiencing.

Nobody responded, so Dicko blew the candle out and lay on the floor, next to Yoler. He felt wide awake, the adrenaline still coursing through his veins, and it seemed like he was staring into the darkness for hours.

*

Dicko's eyes opened when a chill shook his frame. The sound of the wind alerted him even more, and the man sat up and looked around the cabin. The door to the cabin was open by a few inches and the cabinet against it had moved. Either somebody or something tried to get in, or somebody had snuck out and tried to put the cabinet back.

He stood to his feet and could see that dawn was breaking and could see that somebody was missing.

He crept around the cabin, trying not to wake anybody up, and heard the voice of Donald Brownstone.

"What are you doing, Dicko?" he snapped. "Fuck's sake, I'm lucky to have gotten two hours sleep, you dig what I'm sayin'?"

"Somebody's missing."

"What do you mean?" Donald took out his lighter and lit the candle that was on the floor. As soon as the flame lit the cabin up, Donald cried, "Where's Helen?"

"Shit."

The two men moved the cabinet from the door and left the cabin, leaving Grace and Yoler stirring and groaning from the noise. Dawn was breaking and thankfully there was some light to guide the men.

"Donald, wait up!" Dicko called out.

Donald ran through the cluster of trees to their left, heading to the pond, and Dicko tried to keep up with him. There was no one at the pond area and both men could see that the field, and the hill that led up to the burnt-out farmhouse, didn't have a soul on it.

"Where could she be?" The panic was hard for Donald to hide and he was getting more anxious by the minute.

"Maybe she's gone for a walk."

"No." Donald shook his head. "Let's try the woods."

They went through the group of trees again, went by the cabin, and entered the woods. Donald was running and Dicko was struggling to keep up. He yelled at Donald to slow down and warned him about the ditch that Hando had fallen in. The day had begun, but in the woods it was still risky, as the trees hid the sun that was slowly rising. Donald had run ahead and was about ten yards further than Dicko who was finding it difficult to keep up.

Dicko felt like his lungs were on fire and was about to give up running, when he saw Donald, from about twenty yards away, standing still, facing right and looking upwards. Dicko walked in the direction of Donald and was baffled why he suddenly decided to stop running, and once the man dropped to his knees and placed the palms over his face, Dicko feared the worst.

Dicko could see the ditch a few yards on the left and decided to peer down. The two Canavars were still in there, but there was nothing left of Hando, except blood, bones and bits of his clothes. Dicko winced at the thought of such a gruesome death, and made his way over to a distraught looking Donald, who was still on his knees, bent over, and crying so hard that Dicko thought his heart was going to break.

No words needed to be said.

Dicko looked to his right and could see that the thought of life without her son wasn't worth living. She had made a drastic decision, and it was something that broke Donald. The blue rope that she had taken from the cabin had been tied around the thick branch that was nine feet off the ground and a noose had been made and placed around her neck. She must have climbed the tree to get to the branch and then jumped off, but how long had she been swinging?

Dicko walked a few steps by Donald's side and placed his arm on the shoulder of the man that was still on his knees. "I'm sorry, Donald."

Donald shook his head and gazed at the lifeless body of the woman he loved. Her face was colourless and he couldn't imagine what the last minute of her life was like.

Donald gulped and sighed, "I'll cut her down."

CHAPTER FORTY-THREE

Donald climbed the tree and had cut Helen down. Instead of allowing the poor woman's body to drop in a heap to the ground, Dicko stood underneath her, ready to catch the falling corpse.

Once the rope was cut and the body caught, a sobbing Donald climbed down and took her from Dicko's arms.

The two men silently walked back to the camp, under a cloud of melancholy, and when they arrived at the cabin, Grace and Yoler were waiting for them by the steps. Both women placed their hands over their mouths once they clocked Helen in Donald's arms, and started to form tears.

Donald fell to his knees, still holding Helen, and kissed her on the top of her head as the other three helplessly watched.

"I'm sorry," he cried. "I tried everything to keep you and David safe, but ... I failed. I failed miserably."

"It's not your fault," Yoler decided to pipe up. "If anything, Dicko and I should have told you when we first saw Hando, we..."

Dicko placed his hand on Yoler's shoulder as she paused and both hugged. He looked over at Grace. The eighteen-year-old girl stood with her head bowed, sobbing. She had no one left in the world now. She had lost her sister, and now her mother and friend.

Dicko broke away from Yoler and went over to console Grace. This had been his saddest day since burying his son. Even the death of Isobel Washington wasn't as bad as this. They had lost four people in one night. One of them was a child.

Dicko broke away from Grace and knelt by Donald. He rubbed the man's back and told him he was sorry.

Donald nodded and said, "I can't believe this is happening."

"It's surreal," was all that Dicko could manage.

Donald cleared his throat and tried to compose himself. He stood up, prompting Dicko to ask where he was going.

"It's only right she's buried with her son," Donald said.

Dicko nodded. "Okay. I'll get the shovel."

*

It took half an hour to dig a grave and bury Helen and after that, Donald announced he needed to go for a walk. Yoler and Dicko were unsure about his idea, but decided not to talk him out of it. The man appeared mentally unstable and unpredictable. Maybe the walk would do him some good.

He told them that he had a knife with him and that he would be away for about an hour or so. Dicko asked Yoler and Grace if they were hungry. He knew what the answer would be, especially from Grace, but he asked anyway. All three decided to skip an early breakfast and sat on the steps of the cabin and watched the sunrise. No one said a word for minutes and Dicko was the first to break the silence.

"I'll take a walk to the pond soon," he said. "Need to grab a couple of buckets and scrub the inside of the cabin."

"You won't get the blood off with pond water and a tea towel," Yoler scoffed.

"I need to give it a try."

"Waste of time, Dicky Boy."

"Have you got any better suggestions?"

There was silence from Yoler Sanders, and she chose not to react to Dicko's snarling query. Everybody was upset, angry, and emotions were riding high after losing Gavin Betrand, Lisa Newton, David Willis, and now his mother.

"Well, whatever his motives for doing this," Dicko spoke, referring to Hando, "he certainly did some damage."

"At least Hando suffered before he went."

Grace listened to what they were saying, but chose not to respond. She couldn't believe it. So this was done on purpose? By this Hando guy?

Dicko stood up and Yoler asked where he was going.

"I'm going to the pond," he said.

"To wash the blood away?"

"No." He shook his head. "You're right about that. Pond water alone won't shift it. I'm just going for a walk. Need to splash my face."

The man in his forties walked through the trees and wiped his forehead with the back of his hand once he was at the water's edge.

He crouched down and dipped his hands in the glorious icy water and splashed his face. He groaned in delight and wet his face a few more times before standing up straight. He looked past the field and smiled as his eyes clocked the farmhouse. He had only stayed there for a short time, but he had good memories of the place. He liked Simon and Imelda, and when Yoler came along he had a lover that was his first since his wife. He had lost everyone during the beginning, and with Simon and Imelda no longer around, he feared that he would lose Yoler one day. He didn't love her, but he was aware that he liked her more than she liked him.

He crouched down and splashed his face once more and ran his wet hands through his hair and beard. He made his way back to the area where the cabin was based. Once he stepped out of the trees and was out in the spacious part where Grace and Yoler were sitting, he could see that Donald had returned.

Dicko stood near the girls and folded his arms, feeling the cold, and needed to get inside and grab his jacket.

The forlorn group, what was left of them, were tired and weary. Grace especially looked exhausted and had only managed to drop off for an hour before the Canavar intrusion that took the lives of Gavin, Lisa, David, and, indirectly, Helen Willis.

"I'm leaving," Donald suddenly blurted out. He looked up to see the reaction of the three, but there was no emotion on the faces of any of them.

"Where are you going?" Yoler was the first out of the three to speak.

Donald shrugged his shoulders. "No idea. Anywhere away from this cursed place." Donald looked around and suggested, "Why don't we all just go?" His query was greeted with silence, so he added, "We have a van. We have food. Let's start somewhere new."

"I don't mind," said Dicko. "I've been moving around since this shit started. Another move won't bother me. Worst comes to the worst, we can sleep in the van."

"Isn't it dangerous to be out on the road, though?" Grace spoke up, unsure whether she liked the idea.

"Of course it is." Donald ran his fingers over his face. Tiredness was crippling his body. "But with the meat wagons out of the way, it won't be as bad. We'll be fine. We won't travel far."

"Where are we gonna go?" Grace asked. "Down south to London? Up north to Scotland?"

Donald groaned, "I don't know yet. Any suggestions?"

"Just drive and see what happens." Yoler smiled after her sentence. "Let's just get the hell out of here."

Grace nodded in agreement. Her mother's body was just yards from her, at the side of the cabin, but leaving her wasn't something that bothered her. She was gone. She wasn't coming back.

"Let's try and get some rest," said Dicko. "And then we'll move the tins into the van and fuck off somewhere ... anywhere. I'll take a walk to the van and see if it's okay, make sure it's still there," he joked.

All agreed with Dicko's suggestion, and Paul Dickson walked into the woods and told them that he'd be back in ten to twenty minutes. Yoler asked if he wanted some company, but he told her no and that they should all get some rest.

The van had turned out to be fine. It was still hidden, and Dicko returned to the cabin. He pushed the cabinet against the door once it was shut and was the last person to lay down his head.

153

CHAPTER FORTY-FOUR

He had no idea of the time, but Donald was the first to wake, and within ten minutes everybody was up. A walk to the van was achieved and Dicko insisted on driving. Grace was nervous about being on the road, being out in the open, but Donald bluntly told her that being in the woods had hardly been a success.

They were all crammed in the front. Not one person wanted to be in the back of the van, and Dicko put this down to paranoia, in case an accident occurred or something else. He looked at the fuel gauge and although there was some gas, he didn't want to waste it by going too far. He wanted to find a place as soon as possible.

The van had been on the road for a good ten minutes and Dicko was struggling to recognise the countryside. He hadn't been this way before.

"Do you know where we're going?" Yoler asked him.

He shook his head as the vehicle hit a sharp bend. The road straightened up and all could see houses in the distance. It was a small place that they could see from half a mile away and it was exactly what they wanted. All they needed to do was find a house and transport the goods in the back of the vehicle to inside a suitable place.

Dicko's eyes narrowed as they neared the entrance of the village, some two hundred yards away, and suddenly brought the van to a stop.

"What's wrong?" Donald asked.

"Take a look," was Dicko's response.

They all stared in confusion, unsure what to do next. There was a barrier at the entrance and vehicles were parked across the road. The vehicles that were creating the barrier slowly parted. And then another vehicle exited the place, in-between the vehicles, and Yoler pointed out that a vehicle was approaching them.

They waited for the vehicle to draw near and it pulled up ten yards from their van. The Ford Sedan's engine was still running as the lone man stepped out of the vehicle. He was dressed in combat gear, appeared to have no weapon on him, and had blonde fuzzy hair, but was clean shaven. He was six feet in height and looked too thin.

Dicko switched the van's engine off and exited the van. The others followed and stood at the front of the van.

"Can I help you?" the driver of the Sedan asked the depleted group.

"I don't know," Yoler spoke up. "*Can* you?"

"You're heading towards our village," the man said. "We tend to be wary of strangers. Especially ones driving vans."

"We're nothing to do with the meat wagons," Dicko said. "If that's what you're implying."

"Heard of them then," the man laughed.

Dicko nodded. "We've heard of them, we've confronted them, and we've killed them. *All* of them."

The thin man's eyes widened with surprise and he scratched at his fuzzy hair. "That's something that'll cheer up the folk back in the village. Especially the ones that have to go out on runs."

"Rest assured. They're all dead."

The man nodded and gazed at the group. He looked to the side and began to chew his bottom lip. He seemed lost in thought. He then straightened his back and smiled at the small group.

"Follow me," he said.

"Why?" Donald asked.

"You need a place to stay. Maybe you could stay with us, but it won't be straightforward. You'll be questioned."

"What makes you think we need a place to stay?" Yoler asked him and folded her arms.

"Don't you?"

There was a silence and they all looked at one another.

"That's what I thought."

The man laughed and got into his car. He turned the engine on, and did a turn in the road and then slowly moved away.

Dicko told them to get back in the van and fired the engine as soon as he was in the driver's seat and pulled away.

CHAPTER FORTY FIVE

The car that Dicko was following was three car lengths away, with both vehicles going at a steady twenty miles per hour. Getting to the village didn't take long, and they could see two guys with shotguns by the entrance, one of many, of the village. It was a small place, a name Dicko had never been to or heard of, despite only being four miles from where they started off in the van. Donald became tetchy as they entered the village. They were told to pull the van up as they got inside, and the four people in the vehicle got out.

A man by the name of Ed asked the four to empty their pockets, drop their weapons, and asked if it was okay to pat them down. Ed was a big man, bald, and looked like a bodybuilder. He was polite with his instructions and neither Dicko, Yoler, Donald or Grace had a problem with them. They did as they were told and began to relax when a female, who introduced herself as Beth, asked them to follow her. They entered a place that used to be a pub and she explained that they used the pub as some kind of reception area for new arrivals.

She told them to stay where they were and they stood in the lounge area of the bar. Beth announced that she was going to get a guy called Derek, who was the second in command, and that they should relax and had nothing to worry about.

"I'll be back in a few minutes," Beth said. She was in her forties, dressed in a red dress, and had a very polite voice.

Dicko was the first to take a seat at one of the tables, and the rest did the same.

"This is a bit dramatic," Donald said. "A bit over the top, don't you think?"

"It's nothing to worry about," Dicko said confidently, folding his arms across his middle. "They can't just let anyone in. They need to check us out."

"Yeah, well, don't mention that we have all that food in the back, you dig what I'm sayin'? What happens if they don't let us in, but rob us?"

"They're gonna check it out eventually."

Donald decided not to respond.

Only a few minutes had passed and the door to the pub opened. A man of average height entered. He was holding a clipboard and seemed different to Beth. His face was deadpan, devoid of emotion, and he sat down at the next table, glaring at the four of them.

He placed the clipboard flat on the table and crossed his legs, pulling out a biro. He asked for their full names, which were given. He wrote down the names on the clipboard and spent a few minutes writing down details such as the features of each one of them. He asked for their height, and then asked what family members they had lost since the announcement last summer, on June 9th.

Neither of them queried why he wanted the information. There were four of them, and just one man with a clipboard, so they didn't feel threatened.

Dicko was the only one that had a question, and wanted something clarified. "Why are these questions necessary, if you don't mind me asking?"

The man was scribbling with his head down, and answered without looking up, "It's kind of a database. After the questions, we will get you medically checked out and you can join us."

"Just like that?"

The man stopped scribbling and looked up. "Just like that. The more people there are, the stronger we become."

"But with food—"

"You don't have to worry about extra mouths to feed," the man sniggered. "When you're checked out, you'll be given a tour. On the other side of the village you'll see that we have acres of land, crops, cattle, poultry."

"Sounds too good to be true," Dicko laughed.

"This was no accident, Mr Dickson. We've all worked hard, and had to endure a bad winter to get here."

After another five minutes of questioning, Derek excused himself and left the pub, leaving the four in the lounge area.

A few minutes later, the door to the pub opened once again, and in stepped a thin man, in his late forties. He had grey hair and a grey beard over his face. From the skin that could be seen, the man looked badly scarred but they weren't recent ones.

He walked towards the four of them and his eyes were fixated on Dicko. They then narrowed and his mouth fell open.

"I don't fucking believe it." The man ran his fingers over his scarred face and a wide smile emerged under his nose. "When I saw your name on Derek's clipboard, I thought … *no way*. I know there's hundreds of Paul Dicksons out there, but ones that are alive?"

Dicko could feel the eyes of Grace, Yoler and Donald staring at him, wondering what was happening.

"I'm sorry." Dicko was perplexed and his eyes narrowed. "Do I know you?"

"It wasn't that long ago, Paul," the man laughed. "We've both got beards now, but I recognise you."

Eyes were still looking at Dicko and he creased his forehead in thought. He had no idea who it was.

"I'm sorry," said Dicko. "I'm none the wiser."

The grey bearded man with the scars took a few more steps forwards and smiled. "Last year, you and your boy were found in some wrecked car. You were brought back to a camp, a caravan park called The Spode Cottage."

Dicko's eyes widened. The penny was finally dropping and he rose to his feet. "No way."

The scarred man knew that Dicko recognised him and said, "Good to see you're still alive, Paul."

Dicko went around the table and stood within a foot of the man and they both embraced, but broke away quickly.

"Can I sit down?" the man asked.

"Of course."

The grey bearded man pulled up a chair and sat at the table. Dicko sat back down and asked him, "How long have you been here? And where's—"

"I've been here a couple of months. And the rest of the crew are fine, last time I saw them."

"Why are you here?" Dicko asked. "I don't get it."

The man could see the other three were baffled and decided to explain in length. "Let me shed some light on what we're talking about."

"Please do." Yoler smiled.

"Paul and I go back a bit. He was with us for a few months before he was taken away from our camp by a guy called Drake. Paul was a bit of a mental case after he lost his son, but he helped out greatly when this Drake and his gang attacked our street. Anyway, our camp and Drake's camp made up and called a truce, but in exchange for Paul. He had killed people close to Drake and we had to give him up."

"So you betrayed Dicko?" Yoler said. It was a story she was already familiar with.

"Is that what you're calling him these days," the scarred man laughed. "Sounds like a porn star." The man cleared his throat and said, "I suppose we gave Paul up to stop further bloodshed. We had kids in our camp as well, you see. We couldn't take the risk."

"I escaped anyway," said Dicko, smiling, thinking back to days gone by.

"Yes, you did. Strangely we went to join Drake for a few months, but something happened and we went back to Colwyn Place at Little Haywood."

"So why are you here?" Donald asked the man.

"I went on a run a few months back." He looked at Dicko and added, "I went out with Terry Braithwaite and a girl called Stephanie. I think we were about ten miles away."

Dicko smiled as he heard the familiar names.

"To cut a long story short, we ran into trouble and they were both killed. I just about managed to escape and ran. A couple of days later, these guys picked me up. I was half dead when they found me."

"How far are we from Little Haywood?"

"About thirty or so miles. Too far." The man began to chew the inside of his mouth and said further, "They probably think I'm dead, like the others."

"Never thought of going back?" Dicko asked.

"I've mentioned it before, but the leader of this place doesn't quite like the idea of his people driving thirty miles to drop me off and then drive back another thirty to get back here. Too dangerous and a waste of petrol. I might go back one day, but I love it here."

"I still think about the old gang," Dicko sighed.

"I do miss the place, and I have been told that I could go, but it'd be on foot. Personally, I'd rather shit in my hands and clap."

"Sorry." Donald held his hands up and asked, "Who *are* you?"

"My fault." Dicko snickered. "This is an old friend. This is Vince. Vince Kindl."

Vince held his hand up to the other three to say hi, and began to talk about the place that was about to be their home.

"You'll like it," Vince told them all. "And Orson is a good guy, although he has his moments."

Dicko looked at Yoler and this was noticed by Vince.

"What is it?" Vince asked.

The four remained silent and Dicko was reluctant to say anything, but Vince persisted with the queries.

"Come on, Paul," he groaned and then chuckled, "Spit it out. Your mother used to."

Dicko could feel Donald and Yoler's eyes glaring at him, with Yoler timidly shaking her head, telling Dicko to keep quiet.

"It's okay," Dicko said to them. "I trust him."

"Well?" Vince Kindl opened his arms to hurry the man up.

"We ran into a few people a couple of months ago, or at least I thought it was that long ago."

"And?"

"A woman called Clare and two other guys entered a place where we were staying and were threatening. They were from this camp. They mentioned Orson. We killed the two guys, and Clare, I think, was taken down by the dead. We had to do it."

A silence enveloped the people in the lounge area of the pub, and it looked like Vince was trying to process the information that had just been given to him.

"Okay." Vince nodded and was lost in thought. "Well, you look like good people to me, and I know you're a good guy, Paul, and I know what you've been through in the beginning of this. I can keep a secret if you lot can. I get it. At the time, you had to do what you had to do. We've all been there."

The four of them looked at one another and Dicko smiled.

"You can trust him," he said.

Vince Kindl stood up and picked the chair up, putting it back where it initially was.

"Once you're checked out, you'll be given a tour by yours truly," he said. "I'll see you guys in a while."

"Where are you going?" Dicko spoke up.

"Gotta be some place." Vince walked over to Dicko. Dicko stood up and both men hugged. "Good to see you're still alive."

Vince broke away from the embrace and exited the pub, leaving Grace, Donald, Yoler and Dicko alone in silence.

"I have a good feeling about this place," Dicko spoke and a smile stretched under his nose.

"He won't say anything, will he?" Yoler wasn't so sure and looked tetchy.

"Trust me." Dicko smiled confidently. "Vince is a good guy. He's not very politically correct, but he has a good heart."

Donald said, "If he blabs about the three that came to that farmhouse, we could be in a heap full of trouble, you dig what I'm sayin'?"

"He won't." Dicko sat back down and look relaxed. "I think, ladies and gentlemen, we may have hit the jackpot."

The four continued to chatter, and a few minutes after, two females turned up. One was an assistant, holding a clipboard, and the other had a small case with her. The woman with the case introduced herself as Dr Lynch and was there to check them out before they went for their tour and were shown their digs.

Grace was first up, and Donald was last to be examined. All four had to strip to their underwear and the men turned away when Yoler and Grace had to take their tops off. Apart from some issues with body odour, some slight malnourishment, dehydration, and Donald's long toenails, Dr Lynch was happy with their health.

"Right," she said, "I'll go and get Vince for your tour and then you can meet Orson. I'll see you around. Oh, and welcome to Uplawmoor Village."

The two disappeared and Grace, Donald, Yoler and Dicko were now buzzing. They were minutes away from becoming a part of a community again, a place that had amenities beyond their wildest dreams, and if they had a doctor on site, what else did they have?

Things were looking good for the four of them.

Life was looking good.

THE END

CHECK OUT OTHER GREAT ZOMBIE NOVELS

DEAD ASCENT
by Jason McPhearson

The dead have risen and they are hungry...

Grizzled war veteran turned game warden, Brayden James and a small group of survivors, fight their way through the rugged wilderness of southern Appalachia to an isolated cabin in the hope of finding sanctuary. Every terrifying step they make they are stalked by a growing mass of staggering corpses, and a raging forest fire, set by the government in hopes of containing the virus.

As all logical routes off the mountain are cut off from them, they seek the higher ground, but they soon realize there is little hope of escape when the dead walk and the world burns.

CHAOS THEORY
by Rich Restucci

The world has fallen to a relentless enemy beyond reason or mercy. With no remorse they rend the planet with tooth and nail.

One man stands against the scourge of death that consumes all.

Teamed with a genius survivalist and a teenage girl, he must flee the teeming dead, the evils of humans left unchecked, and those that would seek to use him. His best weapon to stave off the horrors of this new world? His wit.

CHECK OUT OTHER GREAT ZOMBIE NOVELS

VACCINATION
by Phillip Tomasso

What if the H7N9 vaccination wasn't just a preventative measure against swine flu?

It seemed like the flu came out of nowhere and yet, in no time at all the government manufactured a vaccination. Were lab workers diligent, or could the virus itself have been man-made? Chase McKinney works as a dispatcher at 9-1-1. Taking emergency calls, it becomes immediately obvious that the entire city is infected with the walking dead. His first goal is to reach and save his two children.

Could the walls built by the U.S.A. to keep out illegal aliens, and the fact the Mexican government could not afford to vaccinate their citizens against the flu, make the southern border the only plausible destination for safety?

ZOMBIE, INC
by Chris Dougherty

"WELCOME! To Zombie, Inc. The United Five State Republic's leading manufacturer of zombie defense systems! In business since 2027, Zombie, Inc. puts YOU first. YOUR safety is our MAIN GOAL! Our many home defense options - from Ze Fence® to Ze Popper® to Ze Shed® - fit every need and every budget. Use Scan Code "TELL ME MORE!" for your FREE, in-home*, no obligation consultation! *Schedule your appointment with the confidence that you will NEVER HAVE TO LEAVE YOUR HOME! It isn't safe out there and we know it better than most! Our sales staff is FULLY TRAINED to handle any and all adversarial encounters with the living and the undead". Twenty-five years after the deadly plague, the United Five State Republic's most successful company, Zombie, Inc., is in trouble. Will a simple case of dwindling supply and lessening demand be the end of them or will Zombie, Inc. find a way, however unpalatable, to survive?